I0760261

SMOKES

A NOVEL

GENE UPCHURCH

This is a work of fiction. Names, characters, places, and incidents either are the product of the author's imagination or are used fictitiously. Any resemblance to actual persons, living or dead, events, or locales is entirely coincidental.

Firebrand Publishing publishes in a variety of print and electronic formats and by print-on-demand. For more information about Firebrand Publishing products, visit https:// fi rebrandpublishing.com

ISBN 978-1-941907-69-6 (*hardcover*)
ISBN 978-1-941907-70-2 (*eBook*)
Published by Firebrand Publishing
Printed in the United States of America

For
Anne Piercy

the most enthusiastic fan
a writer could hope for

PROLOGUE

PRESENT DAY. RURAL NORTH CAROLINA

The townsfolks simply woke up one morning, and there they were.

Ten boxcars, different colors, the names and emblems of various railroads painted on their sides. But now the paint had faded and they were covered in leaves and tree limbs and the debris of neglect, their steel wheels rusting and the dull orange runoff streaming onto the rails and rotten cross ties.

They had been there for years; nobody could remember for exactly how long.

Some of the local graffiti artists added their touches over the years, hoping their artwork would be seen by millions as the boxcars traveled the country's rails.

But the boxcars hadn't moved.

How they got there and why they were brought there had made for interesting gossip in the tiny community back in these woods in the foothills of these mountains. But, as time went on, people lost interest and the boxcars, a once mildly interesting attraction, were now a part of the landscape itself, like the trees and streams, dead possums on the road, and the abrupt but familiar sharp bangs of hunters' guns echoing through the valley.

They were at the end of a line that once served a coal mine that had long since played out, sending its workers into unemployment and poverty. After a decade of nobody caring, the mayor made a lot of noise calling the abandoned boxcars being "a blight on the community." The removal of this scourge became the central theme of his pitiful campaign.

All the political noise forced the railroad to send out a man to see what needed to be done. But in all honesty, the purpose of the task assigned to him was to figure out how to do nothing, spend no money, and make sure the noisy mayor didn't get re-elected (while making everyone feel good about it).

The railroad man told the mayor that the wooden trestle over the tiny Toe River had rotted so much that it wouldn't support the weight of a train and no money would be spent to fix the trestle just to pull these worthless cars out.

Also, the railroad man's inspection concluded that the axles on most of the car's steel wheels were so rusted that they probably wouldn't turn.

So, here the boxcars sat, no hope of ever moving again or ever leaving this place.

Several attempts had been made over the years by some of the local geniuses to break into the boxcars to steal anything valuable.

They tried every trick they knew. Shotgun blasts to the military grade locks. Welders' torches to the sides and roofs. Crowbars wedged into the seams where the cars were joined. They had considered dynamite but nobody knew where to get any or how to set it off if they did.

Nothing worked and everyone lost interest.

But not the railroad man.

He returned on his day off, unrecognizable without his customary railroad uniform with the company's logo stitched over his pocket, and not driving his official automobile. He was with two of his friends, one whom knew how to work the acetylene torch. The railroad man maneuvered a massive pickup truck awkwardly down the slope next to the tracks since there was no road nearby.

The railroad man had been intrigued by these boxcars and had seen the scars on the locks and sides of cars created by all the failed efforts to break into them.

But he knew about boxcars. He knew where the metal was thinnest and where a powerful torch could burn through the metal creating a hole large enough for them to see inside.

They went to work, the torch operator with his welders' mask and thick leather gloves, cutting a circular hole into the end of one of the boxcars where the railroad man said was the most vulnerable.

But even at this spot the metal was so thick it took the man and his torch nearly two hours to cut a two-foot circular hole.

As the final inch was burned, a thin puff of aromatic smoke snuck out of the cracks opened by the torch as the railroad man used a ball peen hammer to knock loose the piece of round metal that had been cut out.

As he did flames spat violently from the hole as air rushed into the boxcar for the first time in decades, knocking the railroad man backwards onto the boxcar's coupling.

Whatever was inside had been ignited by the torch setting the innards of the boxcar on fire. They had no extinguisher to squirt into the hole so the railroad man and his friends were defenseless as yellow flames shot out like a broken gas main and smoke seeped out of the cracks around the roof of the boxcar.

They had no idea what was inside but they knew it might explode. They looked at each other, ran for their truck, and disappeared.

An hour later a twelve-year old on his bike stopped and stared at the boxcars. They had always been a part of his entire young life and nothing had ever changed until today.

He stared and stared, afraid to go closer.

Smoke oozed out of the end of one of them. He cycled quickly home and told his mom. She didn't believe him entirely but called down to the fire station where her brother, an assistant chief, was hanging out.

The little fire department rarely got any calls so the brother excitedly sounded the alarm. He jumped into Engine One – an ongoing joke in the town since there was only one engine -- and roared out of the station with lights and sirens toward what he hoped was an inferno. His colleagues got the call on their pagers hoping the boring week would be interrupted by a day of drama. They sped to the scene, the red lights on the dashboards of their pickups flashing with great urgency.

The boxcars were difficult to get to because the tracks were in an isolated spot and the volunteer firefighters hadn't really trained for anything of this magnitude. But this is what their pickups with huge tires and loud engines were made for, so they cut through the woods and ditches and made their own road. Engine One, meanwhile, parked on the nearest road, its huge diesel engine idling and red lights flashing with intensity, completely useless because the tracks were out of reach of its hoses.

The assistant chief caught a ride through the woods on the back of one of the pickups which cut a path through the underbrush and over the fallen and rotten trees, its little red light still flashing even though the only traffic to shoo out of the way were squirrels and possums.

They arrived at a disappointing scene. The

smoke was now a curly wisp lazily exiting the hole in the boxcar, swirling briefly and then disappearing. Even though there was certainly no inferno now, the black smudge above the hole proved there had been one not long before.

The assistant chief was the so-called on-scene commander, so it was his duty to sneak up to the boxcar and determine their next steps. Even though he got a lot of advice from the other volunteers they waited patiently for him to take the lead.

He crawled up onto the coupling apparatus between the boxcars. He couldn't see in so he dispatched his colleagues up the hill to Engine One to bring back a ladder. They positioned it on a cross tie then cranked it up so the top of it was a few feet above the smoky hole. At least this was something they had practiced.

The assistant chief climbed up the ladder until he was head-high with the hole.

No flames. Just a little smoke which smelled sweet—unlike the acrid smell of a house fire or the unique smell of a forest fire or even the metallic smell of a burning electric car which sometimes burst into flames for no reason and were impossible to extinguish before the cars simply melted on the road.

He turned on his huge firefighter flashlight, stuck it in the hole, and swung the powerful beam back and forth through the inside of the smoky boxcar.

The packages nearest the hole had burned up and now smoldered. The rest of the car appeared to be packed with boxes that had remained untouched by the fire.

He squinted to see what was printed on the boxes, and aimed the beam of his powerful light on one of them.

Chesterfield

Then he squinted at the smaller print.

Always milder.

Better tasting.

Cooler smoking.

And, then he knew what he'd found.

But he had so many questions! Nobody remembers seeing all these boxcars shoved into this forgotten place, no recollection of a noisy locomotive doing its job or the excitement of a train coming through.

Why are they here?

CHAPTER ONE

THIRTY YEARS EARLIER

The old man owned everything he could see.

He sat on his porch in a white rocking chair, a smoldering stogie wedged between two left fingers, a glass of rye whiskey and ice sweating on the chair's right armrest as he watched the dusk begin to drape his empire.

The porch of his comfortable white house overlooked his mountains and his lake in his valley where a light fog was forming as the day cooled. He truly owned nearly everything he could see except for the tiny village in the distance where the lights of an early evening began to wink at him.

On most evenings, he had few worries or concerns.

But this evening he was unsettled, not sure if he should be worried as he wrestled with his reflections of the day's events.

Two of his huge horses, Daisy and Strawberry, had been hitched to one of his elegant carriages as he drove them over fifteen miles of narrow and winding carriage roads carved out of the hills and valleys on the thousands of acres he owned. The roads wrapped around the steep hills with switchbacks and sharp turns that challenged the horses and stimulated and thrilled their driver.

He reveled in the power of the horse team, siblings from a rendezvous between a Clydesdale and a Dutch breed of driving horse, and their willingness to go where he directed.

Most of all he loved the moments when he would pull them up and there was no sound except their easy breathing and their pawing at the cinders that made up the roadbed. In these moments he sat in his carriage and embraced the calm and quiet the damp woods shared with him.

It rained overnight, so everything in the forest was fresh and damp. The cinders and rocks of the roadbed might've been treacherous for a person on foot but the horses hardly noticed. Water dripping off the leaves of the massive oak trees in his forest made it sound like it was still raining but the sky above was clear.

The horses knew it before he did.

Daisy first put her ears back and broke stride. Then Strawberry pulled up and reared back on her massive back legs, head shaking from side to side.

Two men rushed out of the bushes, one from each side of the road, and ran toward the elegant carriage.

As they rushed toward him and his thrashing horses, the old man pulled his forty-four-caliber long barreled pistol from under the blanket on the carriage's leather seat.

He fired once into the air and then fired again over the head of one of the attackers as the horrifying whizz of the massive bullet passed within inches of ending the attacker's life.

The horses lurched forward in panic trying to escape the explosive sounds of the gunfire. The carriage jerked but the old man held his balance.

The attackers were unprepared and completely stunned to be fired upon. They whipped around and fled into the dank woods, their arms flailing as they broke through the underbrush to escape a likely death or maiming that could be caused by such a large-caliber bullet..

The old man stepped from the carriage, speaking softly as he stroked the long heads of his beautiful horses to calm them. They were jittery from the encounter and stamped their hooves dramatically into the roadbed's cinders to show their displeasure.

As the old man caught his breath and slowed his racing heart, he thought for a moment.

He was the richest man in the state, by far, but never thought he needed a bodyguard, even though his corporate people warned him for years he could become a target for kidnapping. *Who would bother me on my beloved mountain, on these quiet and wonderful little roads, far from anyone who would harm me?* he always asked himself and the others in the corporate headquarters who looked at one another with concern and resignation. He always won the argument that such precautions were a waste of money and resources.

After some time had passed, Daisy and Strawberry remained nervous and he was still a bit shaken himself so he decided to go straight home. It took several minutes to wheel the reluctant horses around in the carriage road so they were pointed toward the barn where they eagerly headed.

The horses had now been cared for by the stable boys and his evening meal had been prepared and served by his house staff, one of whom would join him later in the evening in his quarters, happy to earn the bonus that was sending her son to the nearby community college. The old man dined alone as usual at his seat at the head of an enormous table that had been planed from a hundred-year-old oak tree where he ate a three-course meal with a bottle of red wine from his three-thousand bottle cellar.

And, now he sat on his porch, waiting, fretting.

Off in the distance, through the chilly night air, came the faint sound of a train whistle.

Finally, thought the old man.

On that train would be his man Jenkins making his weekly trip from the old man's cigarette factory in Durham, his leather case filled with correspondence that needed the attention of the old man but more importantly the ledgers that would tell the old man how much money he'd made that week.

The old man didn't trust the telegraph operators and couriers to keep his secrets and he'd never figure out a way to get his information each week unless poor Jenkins did it personally.

Every Friday morning while the old man spent his summers relaxing in the cool mountains, Jenkins boarded a train waiting for him on the siding where the factory's cigarettes were loaded into boxcars for delivery to the addicted smokers in New York and Pennsylvania. The train was a "loaner" from the railroad to the old man, one of the railroad's best customers. It had a diesel electric, one of the newest locomotives on the market, a club car where Jenkins was the lone passenger, and a caboose with a conductor.

The trip took all day and the old man had enough clout that the freight trains would be sidetracked while Jenkins' train rumbled through the middle of the state and began the winding and gradual incline up the foothills into the mountains. Jenkins' train could go no further than Black Mountain so it was there that he transferred to a local train that took him to the small village at the bottom of the old man's mountain.

When he reached the village, he was greeted by the old man's Lincoln Continental and the elegant car's driver, a man named Smitty who drove him up the winding road to the old man on the porch.

As Jenkins got out of the car, Smitty as usual handed him a sheet of paper which Jenkins shoved into the inner pocket of his suit coat, a safe place until he could study it later. Jenkins counted on the driver to keep him updated on who the old man met with, who he talked with on the phone and the contents of any telegrams that made their way to the old man's front door. Smitty could always count on finding a large envelope on the backseat filled with cash.

Jenkins spent all week managing the old man's affairs, organizing the books and settling personnel problems. And then, on Friday, he made the trip to the porch where they promptly entered the house and spread out the week's paperwork on a large desk. They would work late into the night. At dawn on Saturday Jenkins would return home, usually arriving in time for dinner with his frustrated wife and children.

This was Jenkins' life.

It never occurred to the old man that Jenkins

spent two days away from his family every week or that two engineers and a conductor suffered likewise, nor did he ever calculate the enormous cost of the train trip.

He didn't care because the cash was rolling in so fast that he and Jenkins could barely keep up.

The cigarette business had never been better. He had two factories that were now automated and could spit out millions of filtered cigarettes every hour.

He invented a mechanical system to roll them perfectly so the spoil rate was miniscule. They were perfect.

He also had developed an auction system that bought bright leaf-cured tobacco from farmers who could count on a profit of a thousand dollars for every acre of tobacco they grew. A farmer with forty acres was a rich man with new tractors and a gleaming Buick to drive to church. Everybody was a winner.

It was now ten years after the end of World War II and the old man and some of his cronies and competitors were profiting from an audacious vision that would eventually guarantee them enormous wealth.

During the war they gave their cigarettes to

the soldiers and airmen overseas. Gave them away. They paid for the manufacture, shipping, distribution, everything. They knew the nicotine in the cigarettes was addictive and the soldiers would be hooked when the war inevitably ended.

They returned home willing to pay top dollar for a pack of Lucky Strikes or Chesterfields and the old man had a production system ready to meet their needs.

The old man's next vision was cynical, to say the least, but his plan was to endow one of the state's leading hospitals so it could treat the millions of his customers whose lungs eventually would be destroyed by his products. It was the least he could do, he thought, and the tax advantages would be enormous.

On this summer evening, the impatient old man sat in his home office, his mind filled with visions and big plans and troubling memories of the day's attack, and an exhausted Jenkins, whose briefcase was filled with the minutiae of the week's business.

The old man would look at every line of the ledgers which showed where the money was coming from and where it was going and how much was left over. He focused on the big numbers, the revenue from the distributors in the Northeast, but he was a master of understanding the costs because that's how a business becomes successful. He looked at the largest of the invoices and the payroll and both were always pretty consistent.

"You need to look at these," Jenkins finally said when he sensed the old man was growing weary of numbers.

He pushed a stack of letters toward the old man who opened them one by one. The letters, addressed to his senior accountant and sales managers, were from angry distributors in Pennsylvania, New York and New Jersey. He sat forward in his chair and adjusted the lamp on the table. Jenkins had read them so he was prepared for what was next.

"What do you make of this?" the old man asked Jenkins.

Jenkins paused before answering. Each letter was a grievance about being shorted on inventory but was invoiced for the full amount. And they were demanding refunds.

"I'm still working on it," Jenkins said. "I've personally tracked the entire process from when the product is made until it's loaded on our trains.

Somewhere along the way the product is disappearing from locked and sealed freight trains."

The old man looked at him with frustration.

"Ok, Jenkins, let's do the refunds, send 'em some bonus inventory to show our good will," the old man said. "And then do whatever it takes, hire whoever you need and find out who's stealing our stuff. Because that's what's happening."

The old man then closed one of the ledgers, and leaned back in his chair.

"I need to tell you something," he said to Jenkins.

CHAPTER TWO

Every day was the same.

Bert and Eileen woke next to each other in the small bed they shared in an unpainted shotgun house they didn't own.

They had no alarm clock to wake them at five thirty in the morning where it was still dark on the mill hill even in the stifling early mornings of summer when the sun appeared sooner. They didn't own a clock or a tv. They had a toaster and a coffee pot.

Coffee at their breakfast table was thin and weak and barely hot. If they were fortunate enough to have eggs Eileen would boil one that they cut in half and each would add a half to their spartan lunch pails with a small slice of cheese, half an apple, and a piece of ham if they could afford it.

They would leave together, but never hand in hand, and walk silently down the dark gravel street that the mill owner sprayed with used machinery oil to keep down the dust. There were probably better ways to manage but paving the street was never an option for the mill owner. One of his assistants had done the math and the only cost of using the oil was the cost of labor to spray it on the street, so that became the solution.

The oil clung to the soles of their old shoes. In the hot summer sun it turned from a thick paste to a liquid. They walked in the ditch or along the edges of the gravel as they made their way to the end of the street and the back gate of the mill where a security guard with a baton glared at them and sometimes made them open their lunch pails to make sure they weren't bringing cigarettes or liquor to work.

Once they were through the gate, they said goodbye without a kiss and often without a glance. Eileen entered the massive brick building with a throng of other women, all walking slowly, heads down, no smiles, gossip, or chatter. Bert walked around the corner of the building to the loading dock where he stowed his lunch pail and waited with some other men.

Moments later, the whistle blew, and the looms started turning. They were powered by electricity but still required a multitude of women to manually hurl the shuttles back and forth pulling the threads tight in the cotton sheet. A missed pass with the shuttle would cause a flaw in the product.

After four and a half hours of a mind-numbing, hopeless morning the whistle blew a short toot and the looms slowed to a halt. The women took their pails to the break room and silently ate their lunches. If the weather was nice they would sit outside at some picnic tables. They coughed as they ate because as they worked they breathed in the cotton dust that floated like a white haze. It tickled all the time and was worse when they ate.

After thirty minutes the whistle sounded its sorrowful note to return to work and the looms began turning, demanding the women pass the shuttle back and forth for another four and a half hours.

Bert and Eileen slowly walked home together every day in exhausted silence, their bodies slumped from the hours of labor. If they were lucky the afternoon newspaper would be waiting on their porch unless the paperboy was running late, distracted by a pickup football game or some girl. When the paper came on time and the weather was nice, they would divide up the sections and read every word while sitting on their front porch with its view of another house just like theirs across the oily street.

They only worked a half day on Saturdays, which was also payday. After the whistle blew to set them free, they lined up at the cashier's office for their week's pay. Like all the employees, Bert and Eileen's house was owned by the mill which deducted the rent from their pay. They paid other deductions—for their meager purchases from the company-owned grocery and for the company doctor when they were sick. By the time all the deductions were added up there was usually very little left.

This was their life.

It never changed.

Eileen hated it.

On the hot summer nights, with the windows of their pathetic little house open to stir some air, the only scent was not of roses or lavender like in Eileen's dreams but the pungent odor of the oil that kept her street free of dust.

Eileen lay on her back on these nights, hands folded across her stomach, listening to Bert snore, and silently wept.

Is this all there is to my life?

She stayed frustrated and restless.

She didn't need champagne but she needed something. She didn't know what.

Her frustration was compounded by Bert who seemed satisfied to load trucks and eat meager meals and live in an unpainted house they would never own.

In the miserable darkness of the nights next to Bert, she agonized that she had broken a vow to herself when she was a teenager in a hospital bed, a vow that her life would become better than that dreadful moment with the blinding lights surrounded by the incessant sounds of the emergency room. At that moment, she felt pain unlike anything she'd ever experienced. She didn't think she was dying, but wasn't certain.

And now, as she lay next to Bert, she had flashbacks of her teenaged body tethered to tubes and machines and remembered how she didn't feel the needles or sticky pads attached to her body. In spite of the pain, she experienced a sense of peace. There would be no knocks at her door. No one would hurt her, or rob her, or wake her with drunken threats.

As these memories chased the sleep away night after night, she would often gasp at the horrors that always began with the first drink she served at twelve years old.

It happened one night when her mother was in the back bedroom with a guy and the door was closed and locked. It was about two in the morning and the banging on the front door woke her up. Eileen didn't want to bother her mother and knew she probably would get a whipping for opening the door.

But the banging wouldn't stop. It was a customer and he had three dollars for a five-dollar shot.

Eileen took his three dollars and he helped himself. He looked at her like he might want to help himself to something else but thought better of it and quickly left through the open front door into the dank Durham night.

Eileen reflected in agony about how she grew older and became more involved with the family business. Her mother learned to trust her and Eileen became confident she could handle nearly any drunk, cheapskate or troublemaker who came through the front door. Most of them were just old drunks and easy to handle.

The house was at the end of Gurley Street, a dead end near downtown with a dirt path through the woods that customers used as a short cut and escape route. Gurley Street had never been paved because the slum lords who owned the houses didn't see the need to pay the city to provide their tenants with that luxury. The city came through once a year and scraped the rocks on the street to smooth out the potholes and hosed it down with oil. Their customers would traipse through the gunk and track it into the house.

Mr. Sorrell didn't own the house but he collected rent for the owner. Every Friday he parked his Buick in the driveway and collected $110 and always gave a receipt. He would leave the car there while he walked to three other houses to collect from them. Everybody was always home on rent day; they knew a single missed payment meant Mr. Sorrell would change the locks until they paid.

Mr. Sorrell once told Eileen's mother that he'd heard a rumor she was running a liquor house and that if he caught her he'd have the sheriff evict her. She told him he didn't need to worry about her selling liquor.

Eileen became a big part of the business. One of her jobs after school was to get supplies from the A&P, a three-mile bus ride from Gurley Street. With the money her mother gave her, Eileen would get plastic cocktail cups, coke and soda water, even though most of the customers didn't require a mixer, then struggle on the bus home carrying the paper bags.

Starting around seven, the front room would fill with a constantly changing collection of six to eight men at a time drinking whisky and rum in Eileen's plastic cocktail cups talking among themselves or just sitting in a chair staring at their drink.

The price was the same for everybody: five dollars for a two-finger shot, a splash of coke or soda included if you wanted it. Most of them wore smelly work clothes with their name stitched over their right pocket and their employer's name stitched on the left. These were working people, happy to have a job they hated. Eileen always noticed how sad and exhausted they looked when they entered but how a visit to the front room always made them seem a little happier by the time they left.

The men always looked at Eileen's breasts especially as she started to mature into a woman. Some would brush up against her or touch her thigh. She ignored them with ice cold detachment, but inside she was terrified. Sometimes they'd ask if she wanted to play and she ignored that too. After a couple of drinks one of them offered her mother his weekly paycheck if he could lay with Eileen for a few minutes in the back room. Her mother put her finger in his face and told him if he laid with anyone it would be *her* and it would cost him more than a week's pay.

The front room was usually quiet but sometimes there would be an argument over something. Loud voices and obscenities would fill the house. Sometimes there would be pushing and shoving and sometimes a fist would be thrown. But the customers knew better than to get too rough and especially knew their dispute couldn't spill on to the front porch where a nosy somebody might call Mr. Sorrell.

"Girl," one of them said one night, "you shorted me on my drink."

Eileen didn't know what to say.

"Make it right," he demanded. "Give me a free drink!"

His voice was getting loud. Her mother was in the back room but heard his voice and came to the front room with an empty half-gallon glass Aristocrat bottle and smashed him in the back of the head. He skulked out, and never came back.

Nobody ever called the cops. If things got too rough her mother would send Eileen next door to fetch Jim, a big man who worked at the Firestone downtown. He didn't drink so he didn't come to the house unless he was fetched by Eileen to bring his tire iron.

These were moments that Eileen hated. She couldn't stand the yelling and conflict. It made her want to run away. There was no privacy in her house; there was always somebody in the only bathroom. When they started yelling her mother would scream at them to shut up and behave. Eileen would cover her ears and escape to her little room in the back.

The last customer would leave around two and Eileen would struggle out of bed four hours later and try to go to school. School wasn't much of a priority in her house but Eileen had enough sense to know that she didn't want to serve liquor the rest of her life. She slept at school, sometimes in a quiet stairwell near the auditorium, but mostly by accident in class. If she snored the teacher would wake her and sometimes send her to Mr. Hedrick, the kindly old principal. He wanted to know why she slept in class and not at home. Eileen lied and told him that her mother worked late and woke her when she came home. Mr. Hedrick wasn't sure what to do so he told her to quit sleeping in class and disturbing the other kids.

It was late on a Friday night that a stranger came through the door. It wasn't too unusual for somebody new to come to the house but everyone was always wary in case Mr. Sorrell had sent a spy.

The night had wound down early for a Friday and Eileen's mother had stepped out for a few hours without saying why. The stranger looked around as if looking for someone and asked how much for a whisky. Eileen told him, took his money and poured him a drink. The stranger didn't sit but took his drink in a single swallow and asked for another.

Eileen came over with the bottle. As she reached down to pour his shot, he grabbed her arm and pulled her to him, wrapping his arm around her throat, the drink still in his hand. He swigged the drink in a single swallow, dropped the cup on the floor and pulled a small knife from his pocket.

He put the point to her throat.

"Who else is here?" he asked, the awful smell of the liquor on his breath.

"You never know," she said defiantly, trying to pull away from him.

He hesitated for a moment, then stuffed a filthy handkerchief in her mouth and dragged her to the back of the house into the dark room that was hers. He flung her on her little bed and held her down as he pulled off her skirt and tore off her underwear. She squirmed but he held her down with one hand as he dropped his pants with the other. She closed her eyes tight, in disbelief of what was happening.

Suddenly the stranger groaned and Eileen's face was covered with a sticky wetness. The full weight of the stranger was on her, pinning her to the bed but not moving.

The overhead light in the little room flicked on. She opened her eyes and peered over the stranger's heavy body to see Jim and his tire iron. She wiped the sticky mess from her face; it was the stranger's blood. She felt sick.

Jim held an angry look in his eyes. He quietly told her that he could see the attack from his living room through her open window. The stranger was groaning and bleeding on her little bed. Jim pulled him off the bed and dragged him out the back door into the darkness. When Jim came back in a few minutes he told her that he pulled the stranger down the dirt path at the end of the dead end and rolled him into the weeds at the side of the path. Somebody will find him, Jim said, or he'll wake up and go away. Eileen had never hugged a man before, but she hugged Jim that night and thanked him.

When Jim left, Eileen decided to leave also, forever.

She didn't have much but she put what she had in an A&P bag and walked out the front door through the oily muck of Gurley Street toward downtown and the bus station, the only place she could think of to go.

She slipped through the door of the old station that smelled of diesel, piss and pigeon shit, and looked around at the small collection of people who looked as exhausted and lost as she did. She slumped at the end of a wooden bench and immediately fell asleep, her head on her chest.

Officer Bob Lewis was on one of the downtown beats and he always stopped by the bus station to run off the homeless guys and vagrants who tried to sleep there. He didn't arrest these folks unless they fought him and he'd give somebody a break if they were especially pitiful or the weather was cold and nasty.

He was the kind of cop you'd want at your wreck, break in or dispute with your neighbor. He was kind and had an easy laugh. He always tried to find a solution that helped everybody. But if you messed with him, you'd go to jail or the hospital. He'd been a cop since he graduated from high school and loved his job. Once a month he was assigned the district that included Gurley Street but never went there. No cop ever just cruised Gurley Street—only if there was a murder or something so heinous Gurley Street couldn't handle it itself.

He spotted the girl on the bench, wearily sliding next to her.

"You know you can't sleep here," he said, "but I'll let you stay if you have a ticket for the bus in the morning."

She looked at him with exhausted, sad eyes. "I can't afford a ticket."

Officer Lewis had seen this sight many times, a runaway girl who'd been abused or hurt with nowhere to go. He knew that once they got away and cleared their heads they usually went home.

"Let me take you home," he said. "I'll break the rules and give you a ride in my cruiser if you promise not to tell anybody."

She thought for a moment, but realized she really had no other choice and nodded.

They pulled slowly onto Gurley Street, his squad car a rare sight in the desperate little neighborhood. Eileen told him her house was the last one of the left and Officer Lewis pulled slowly down the dark street.

Suddenly, out of the darkness, Jim ran toward them, yelling and waving his arms.

A bright flash, and Jim fell face first in his yard.

Officer Lewis reached for his radio. The stranger who tried to rape her stood there in the headlights. Two bright flashes, loud booms, glass exploded and Officer Lewis fell over, his head brushing Eileen's leg, blood pouring onto the floorboard. The squad car lurched forward as Officer Lewis's foot left the brake, stopping with a jolt as it wedged into the ditch in front of Eileen's house.

She screamed, shaking uncontrollably. The stranger walked around to the passenger side of the squad car.

"I can't believe you called the cops," he growled through clenched teeth.

Another bright light, and Eileen stopped screaming.

When Eileen woke, she found herself laying still in the hospital bed.

No one was with her. What she didn't know, couldn't know, was that Jim was already in the morgue and Officer Lewis was two doors down, surrounded by six officers who removed his badge, gun and wallet and placed them in a manila folder. They stood in a silent salute to their buddy before pulling the sheet over his shattered face. They quietly discussed who would call Robin, his wife.

Eileen's pain was unlike anything she'd ever felt. She wanted to scream, but couldn't make a sound or move. The pain rose like a geyser.

At that moment, her brain tangled by pain, brought an unexpected moment of brilliant and surprising clarity as she vowed that her life would never be like this again.

CHAPTER THREE

One afternoon after the mill's whistle finally signaled the end of another soul-shattering day, Eileen waited for Bert just inside the back gate. She usually arrived before Bert because the looms stopped when the whistle blew but Bert's day ended when the last truck had been loaded so his arrival at the back gate was unpredictable.

On this day, Eileen waited alone as always and through the fence she saw two men handing out flyers to the mill workers. This was not unusual; sometimes local politicians or candidates for office would greet the workers and ask for a vote but the mill's security thugs would make them move into the street and off the property.

Other times people would hand out coupons for a local grocery that competed with the mill's store and were run off with a threat of physical harm.

But these men were different. They were dressed nicely in coats, ties and hats and waved their flyers in the air and shouted like carnival barkers.

"American Tobacco is hiring downtown! We need workers like you! Top pay, good benefits, forty-hour weeks!"

Eileen was intrigued and planned to take a flyer on her way out.

Just then, Mr. Baker, the mill supervisor, came storming like a battleship around the corner of the mill flanked by two security thugs. It was off-putting to see him without his suit jacket on. Eileen was certain he'd left it in the office, but she never had seen him without it. He clenched his cigar in his teeth and his face was blistering red.

He got to the gate, pointed with his cigar to the two men from American Tobacco and snarled at his thugs, "Send 'em outta here hurtin'."

The thugs menacingly surged out through the gate, pushing some workers out of the way, and rushed up to the tobacco guys, knocking them to the ground and punching them in the face. When they went sprawling, the wind scattered their flyers in all directions. There was a brief scuffle but the tobacco guys were no match for the thugs and limped away. The thugs returned to Mr. Baker's side and together they retreated into the mill.

Bert arrived as the drama ended. As they left the mill, Eileen picked up a flyer off the ground. It had a few drops of blood on it.

They sat on the porch when they got home, Bert with the front section of the newspaper, Eileen with the bloodied flyer. She read it three times, set it down, then picked it up and read it a fourth.

"We should do this," she said to Bert who looked up from his paper. "What's to lose by going and talking to them? Besides, it might get us out of this shitty place."

"What's to lose?" Bert asked. "Our jobs, for one. You saw what they did today. The mill's not gonna look kindly on any of us who talk to another company. Besides, when can we go? We never have a day off or a vacation."

There was a tense silence. Eileen seethed at the thought that Bert was so lacking in ambition that he wouldn't even consider an opportunity. She wanted to scream.

Bert returned to the newspaper, ending the conversation.

Eileen stared at him, shaking with anger.

Finally, she walked over to where he sat, and stood in front of him.

"You're going," she said menacingly, glaring down at him. "Something has to change."

A week later, Bert called in sick and walked to the bus stop at the end of the oily street he called home. He rarely went downtown but the bus driver was helpful and told him where to get off and how to get the American Tobacco Company from there.

He followed the driver's directions to a massive brick building, bigger than anything he'd ever seen with towering smokestacks advertising the company's cigarettes and trucks and people moving everywhere. Everything looked new and clean and exciting.

After a moment, he saw a sign that said, "Now hiring!" so he walked through the door, and, for the first time in his life, entered a room with air conditioning. The room buzzed with activity. The people were nicely dressed and smiling and there even was some laughter from one of the offices. A woman came up to him wearing a friendly smile and asked if he was looking for a job.

"Well," Bert said, "I'm certainly interested in talking about one."

The woman took him to a spartan little office and they talked for a long time about Bert's current job and life on the mill hill. The woman never frowned while listening about his skills, which were few.

"We have dozens of jobs for you," the woman said. "Here, you work a regular shift five days a week, you get vacation time and we pay most of your medical costs. Pick the job you want and start as soon as you want. Live where you want, shop where you want."

Bert looked over the list of jobs, but it was overwhelming.

"Here, let me help. We have openings on the loading dock but we really have a desperate need for workers on our train operation."

Bert stopped looking at the list and looked at the woman.

"Go on," he said.

"We use our own trains to haul our product down to the main line," she said. "Your job wouldn't be to load them but to escort them and make sure the cars don't get tampered with while they're waiting to be hooked up to the big trains on the main line."

She thumbed through a thick book and ran her finger down a row of figures. She told him the pay. It was three times what he made at the mill.

"Is that ok?" the woman asked, a frown on her face as if she was worried it wasn't enough. "And, oh, I almost forgot. We have a hard time filling these jobs because the trains on the main line are unpredictable and sometimes you'll have to spend the night down there. When you do, you get time and a half and the next two days off."

He couldn't believe what he was hearing.

"When can I start?" he asked.

After the first month of his new pay, Bert and Eileen decided she didn't need to work at the mill or anywhere for that matter. They moved their meager belongings out of the unpainted house on the oily street and into a small rented cottage in a nice neighborhood where houses were painted, streets were paved and sounds of children laughing at a nearby park could be heard from their porch.

Bert was gone a lot with his new train duties.

Eileen took in some sewing work to pass the time. It wasn't much but better than whipping a shuttle through a loom six days a week.

One afternoon at her sewing machine, she started sobbing, the kind of crying that comes from deep within a soul as if the body is trying to flush out something hidden, seeking a release.

Her hands were shaking. She couldn't stop sobbing.

What's wrong with me?

She went to the front porch, hoping a breath of air would help and also hoping the neighbors wouldn't see her having this crisis.

What's wrong with me?

CHAPTER FOUR

When the old man leaned back in his chair, Jenkins already knew what he was going to hear.

Jenkins saw that the old man was alive and well, so he knew the attack had failed. Jenkins was frustrated because he gave his guys bad intelligence or, actually, no intelligence.

How was he supposed to know that the old man kept a gun under his carriage seat?

Without registering a drop of emotion, Jenkins listened as the old man recounted the ambush on the carriage trail including the dramatic reaction of his beloved horses and the gunshot that sent his assailants scrambling into the cover of the mountain woods.

"So, what do you think we should do?" the old man asked Jenkins, who pretended to think deeply about the question. He didn't answer immediately because he was still thinking about the twisted events that had led to this sordid point.

"I need to think about it, Boss," Jenkins said, pretending to be thoughtful. "I wonder what their motive was."

Jenkins knew exactly that the motive was a series of unexpected and terrifying developments on one of his weekly and tedious trips to the mountains.

After several hours of pouring over the documents and mail on that trip, gleefully tallying the revenue for the week, the old man surprised Jenkins with a question.

"What do these companies do for us?" he asked, pointing his finger at the names of several companies on the page of one of the ledgers.

It was very unusual for the old man to have an interest in any details. Jenkins had always made sure that was *his* job and that the books the old man saw were clean and didn't provoke any questions. He managed the hiring and firing and all the other nuts and bolts of running the company and shared details on a strict need-to-know basis, which included the old man.

Jenkins looked at the company names under the old man's finger, bile rising in his throat.

None of the three companies were the old man's largest vendors, nor the smallest. They were clustered together on a page full of mid-sized companies that provided a variety of supplies and services to the cigarette company. On other pages were listed the names of three other companies that the old man hadn't seen. Yet.

Jenkins felt the blood drain from his face when he read the name of Amalgamated Machinery Incorporated under the old man's finger.

Like many corporations, the headquarters of Amalgamated Machinery Incorporated were in Manhattan, just around the corner from Wall Street and an easy walk to the post office on Hanover Street and the local branch of Chase Manhattan Bank.

The headquarters of Amalgamated, however, were less ostentatious than most.

The entire contents of its headquarters were stored in a cigar box in the upper right-hand drawer of the desk of a junior attorney in a mid-sized law firm. The box contained deposit slips, a rubber endorsement stamp with Amalgamated's bank account number embossed on it, and a key to a small letter box at the post office.

Once a month, the junior attorney walked from his firm's offices to Hanover Street and retrieved an envelope from the post office box. From there it was just a few blocks to Chase where he would remove the contents of the envelope at a desk in the bank's lobby, stamp the back of the check, and deliver it with a deposit slip to the teller's cage. Once a quarter he withheld an agreed-upon amount from that month's deposit, his compensation for managing a huge corporation.

The partners in his firm had no idea about this arrangement. But the junior attorney included some of his work on his monthly timesheet so the partners actually didn't care and asked no questions. The junior attorney was on his way to becoming a partner, so everyone was happy.

On the 25th day of each month, the junior attorney submitted an invoice to the cigarette company on the embossed letterhead that listed the various machine parts, gizmos and services the company had provided in the previous thirty days, usually amounting to around twenty thousand dollars.

The invoice on its embossed letterhead would arrive three days later in the business office of the cigarette company where a clerk in the accounts payable section of Jenkins' department would present a check to him for approval.

This same monthly ritual was performed at six different companies located throughout the United States.

Twice a year, Jenkins traveled to the local banks that serviced these companies. He was the only person authorized to withdraw funds and he would request a cashier's check for nearly the entire balance in each account, leaving just enough to prevent the bank from levying a service fee.

For several years, Jenkins employed one of his witless nephews to courier the accumulated cashier's checks to the home office of the First Caribbean Bank in Nassau in the Bahamas where a secretive firm, solely owned by Jenkins, was the bank's third largest depositor. Unfortunately, Jenkins's scrutiny of the monthly statements from First Caribbean began to reveal a disturbing trend that the deposits were less than they should be. It was always a mystery to Jenkins's grieving sister that her beloved son disappeared on trip to the Bahamas and was never found.

Jenkins's reflections about his complicated world were interrupted by the old man.

"I want to meet these people," the old man said, rearing back in this chair and lighting another cigar. "Pick out two or three and let's pay them a visit in the next six or nine months. I want to see where our money goes and I think they need to put a face with who's paying them so much money.

"Plus, it wouldn't hurt for me to get out and about. It's easy to lose touch with the real world in these mountains."

Jenkins was silent.

His brain was a jumble.

Jenkins's entire plan actually depended on the old man not paying attention to any details except how much money he was making.

"Well, Jenkins," the old man asked, "did you hear me? You think this is a good idea? Actually, I don't care. I think it is and I want to do it. Make it happen."

Jenkins paused before answering.

"Yes sir, I'll get it going," he said quietly. "I think they'll be happy to see you because you're such an important customer."

He paused again, his mind scrambling wildly for a way to get this under control.

"But please be realistic," he continued. "These people are as busy as you. It might take a few months to get everyone's calendar lined up."

"Hmmf," the old man grunted, squinting at Jenkins, "you can do anything. You can do this, too."

CHAPTER FIVE

Bert loved his new job and couldn't believe his good fortune.

Three or four days a week, he rode the train with its boxcars from the cigarette factory thirty miles through the wooded countryside and tranquil farms to a rail siding on the main line. If everything went according to plan, their train would leave early afternoon and get to the main line when the northbound freight train came through around five.

The cigarette factory owned two aging steam locomotives and a pair of coal cars which were operated by two engineers and two coal handlers, each of whom had seen better days and were nearing retirement. The factory leased the boxcars because there was no way to manage their own as the trains moved up and down the east coast. It also leased time on the spur track that ran from town to the main line from the textile mill which owned it and was supposed to maintain it.

His partner Robbie rode the train with him. Their job was to make sure every cigarette got from the factory and hooked up to a train headed to the nicotine-addicted big cities up north. They were like conductors; one rode in the cab of the locomotive looking backwards and the other hung on the steps of the last boxcar looking forward for anything out of the ordinary.

When it was Bert's turn to ride in the cab, he quizzed the engineer about the locomotive's operation and learned all about the multitude of levers and cranks, the temperature of the boiler and the consumption of coal, where to load the water and what to do when the drive wheels lost traction on an incline.

The cigarette company didn't have a system for communicating with the freight train operators on the main line and no way to communicate with its own trains, so every trip was a crap shoot.

When it worked correctly it was a thing of

beauty. Sometimes the freight train was waiting for them, sometimes they waited for it. The first few trips amazed Bert as he watched the two trains maneuver back and forth to move empty cars onto the siding and move the full ones to the tail end of the freighter.

But it often didn't work right. When they missed the connection with the north-bound freight because they were behind schedule or broken down, the cigarette company's engineer would unhook his locomotive from the cars loaded with cigarettes and head back to town, his whistle fading in the distance as he went home for supper.

That left Bert and Robbie on the siding in the middle of the countryside where nothing was nearby and the dark nights were filled with sounds of things that could be heard rustling in the bushes but not seen.

On these nights, Bert and Robbie didn't sleep. Their job was to take their massive railroad lanterns and long batons and walk the length of the train several times a night, together but on opposite sides of the boxcars, looking for unlocked doors, tampered locks or stowaways hiding underneath.

They never found anything. It was tedious

and Bert missed Eileen but the pay was too good to complain.

There was one aspect of these long nights he absolutely loved.

Twice during the night, express passenger trains passed them, one going north, the other south.

He would listen for them in the darkness and always got excited when he would finally hear their whistles in the distance.

There was something visceral and thrilling about knowing a machine so powerful was heading his way. These were the most modern trains on rails, sleeker than the freight trains and much faster. His excitement grew even greater when the locomotive's headlight first appeared in the distance, a prelude to the sound of the low rumble of the diesels which grew louder and more violent until the train rushed by, gone in a second of wind and sound and shaking of the earth.

Their timing had been particularly lucky for about six weeks until the wheel of a boxcar broke and made them late for the rendezvous with the north-bound freight. They knew they'd missed the connection when they arrived at the siding and the freight train had left them empty boxcars.

After maneuvering all the boxcars full of cigarettes into place and hooking up the empties that had been left for them, the engineer tipped his hat, tooted his whistle, and began the trip back to town with the empty cars. Bert and Robbie were left on the siding as the sun set with railcars full of Chesterfields. They settled in for the night in some chairs they had started leaving in the bushes next to the track and built a small fire to keep warm.

A couple of hours later they made their first trip down the track to check on things which were normal as usual.

As they returned to their little encampment, a pair of men stepped out from between the last two boxcars.

Bert and Robbie held up their huge lanterns to shine a light on the strangers.

"Can we help you?" Bert asked nervously as Robbie tightened the grip on his baton.

Bert and Robbie looked at each other nervously. They were dressed way too nicely to hang out on a train siding in the middle of the night. One wore a sport coat and a fedora, the other bareheaded in a tattered and worn sweater and in the light of the lanterns looked like he'd lost a lot of boxing matches.

"We're here on a business trip," the guy in the fedora said, looking sidewise at his colleague. "We're not here to rob or hurt you, but we want to talk."

Bert and Robbie took a step back and made sure the guys saw their batons. But Bert knew these batons were worthless if the guys had guns.

"We wanna buy some smokes," the guy in the fedora said.

Bert said, "There's a general store a few miles from here that sells them."

"Not what I'm talking about," Fedora said. "We wanna buy them from you guys."

The company had instructed Bert and Robbie that a robbery should never be resisted—*Just give the crooks what they want and we'll make more cigarettes tomorrow.* But they had never thought about a situation where somebody wanted to buy cigarettes directly from them.

"Here's the deal," said Fedora. "We're gonna pay you two guys cash for twenty cases. This is between us and none of it goes to the company. Got it?"

Bert and Robbie looked at each other, and nodded.

"So," Fedora continued, "we'll take the cases of smokes from two or three boxcars so nobody can spot they're missing. You get a nice pay day and everybody is happy."

He told them the price and Bert and Robbie looked at each other again in shock. The price was about a month's wages.

"And what if we don't go along?" Bert asked.

"Let's not talk about that option." Fedora said. "You won't like the ending."

With that, Bert and Robbie went to the last three boxcars and used their master keys to open the sliding doors. Fedora and his buddy unloaded twenty cases and stacked them on the gravel next to the train. The buddy used a flashlight to blink three times into the darkness of the woods next to the siding. A pickup truck clambered through the undergrowth and honeysuckle onto the siding where the driver and the two others loaded the cases into the bed of the truck.

Fedora then turned to Bert and Robbie and handed them each a wad of cash.

"Pretty good wages for unlocking some doors,"

he said. "Talking about this to anyone will be dangerous for the two of you."

Fedora continued, grinning. "We plan for this to be an ongoing enterprise and we hope you'll cooperate."

Bert said, "We never know when we're gonna be here. When we're here something's gone wrong and we've missed the freight train."

"That's okay," replied Fedora. "We have our ways of knowing when you're here. We look forward to next time."

With that, Fedora and his buddy squeezed into the pickup's cab with the driver and the truck with its load disappeared into the underbrush.

When it was quiet, Bert and Robbie looked at each other, and at the money in their hands. Bert just stood there, but Robbie counted his.

"Wow," Robbie said. "It's all there."

Bert had never done anything wrong in his life and now he was trapped in a criminal operation that might make him rich or send him to prison. What will happen when the customers at the end of the line up north count their load and realize they've been shorted?

Too early to tell where this was headed.

Two weeks later, they were stranded again

overnight. They sat by their little campfire shivering in the darkness and wondering if their new business partners would emerge. The passenger trains roared past them but Bert was too preoccupied to enjoy the thrill.

Shortly before dawn, the two appeared. Forty cases this time and double the payments.

The train's operation was smooth for another week, then came another night on the siding when Fedora and his buddy emerged around midnight. Another forty cases, same payment as last time plus a little bonus.

As the night went on, and the passenger trains whooshed by, Bert and Robbie talked about their situation.

"We don't have much choice," Robbie admitted.

Bert replied, "I'm actually surprised nobody has said anything about the missing cases. Surely the people on the end of the line realize they're missing some cases and have complained to the company or refused to pay for cases they're missing."

"What does that tell you?" Robbie asked.

"I have no idea," Bert replied.

"It tells me," Robbie said, "that stealing

cigarettes might be easier than we think. It tells me that they don't have a good way of counting their load. There's no security to speak of. I mean, we're the security and we're no good at it."

Robbie chuckled at his own joke.

"So, what're you getting at?" Bert asked.

Robbie thought for a moment.

"I have no idea," he said, smiling in the light of the campfire.

CHAPTER SIX

On a Friday afternoon after they returned from a normal run down to the main line, the rail supervisor called them to his office. *Here it comes,* thought Bert. *They've figured out who's to blame for all those missing cigarettes.*

They nervously entered the supervisor's office who told them to sit.

Instead of firing them, he smiled.

He told them two things.

First, the main line railroad company had installed a new system that allowed it to monitor the location of its freight trains. It would know when its trains passed certain stations and other waypoints and had developed a way for the cigarette company to call them and find out when to expect the north-bound freight train.

The supervisor grinned. "No more overnights in the middle of nowhere waiting for a train that could be anywhere."

Bert and Robbie processed this information. Bert had mildly mixed feelings because he continued to be thrilled with those nighttime passages of the speeding passenger trains, the whistles far off in the night and the occasional payment from Fedora and his buddy made him feel rich. He wondered how Fedora would react.

Before they could absorb this news the supervisor continued.

The engineers and the coal handlers were retiring. Younger engineers were needed who were familiar with the ancient machines and their quirky requirements. The cigarette factory had looked everywhere for candidates but all the engineers were trained on diesel locomotives and weren't about to take a step backwards in their careers to drive an antique thirty miles a day.

"So," the supervisor said, "we want you two to be our engineers. You've been on the trains. You know how they work and how to take care of them. How about it?"

All of this news was more than Bert and Robbie could process. Then the supervisor closed the deal with an offer of a salary, rather than hourly pay, that they couldn't refuse.

So, they became engineers.

Maybe now Eileen will be satisfied, Bert thought.

Bert became the "owner" of the newer of the elderly machines and Robbie took over the operation of the other locomotive which was fifteen years older and constantly in need of repairs. Both locomotives were the 2x4x2 variety, with two small front wheels, four big drive wheels and two small wheels at the rear.

They had bold ideas about ways to improve the operation of the cigarette company's meager rail empire, especially now that they could predict when they needed to get their trains to the main line siding.

They presented their ideas to the supervisor who was grateful that somebody knew what they were doing because he'd never been able to figure out how to make it work better.

They proposed fewer trips with longer trains. The main line railroad balked at first because their trains heading north were already as long as allowed. But they agreed to add a few additional cars, which was a big deal.

They also convinced the supervisor it was unnecessary for them to both be on the same train which increased the efficiency of the operation ever more. The supervisor was delighted.

The months passed easily as Bert and Robbie took turns taking trains down to the mainline. The longer trains and fewer trips meant more time to repair and maintain the old locomotives so they were in service more regularly with fewer cancelled trips and missed rendezvouses at the main line.

The bigwigs at the cigarette factory were thrilled. They could move more product more efficiently and see the results in the bottom line of the ledgers kept in the office of a man named Mr. Jenkins. The supervisor, naturally, was promoted.

The stolen cigarettes were missed by no one. They were a blip on the balance sheet and a minor nuisance for the sales managers.

Bert and Robbie talked about this nearly every day when their trains were back at the factory and they had a few rare minutes together.

"I wonder," Bert said on this day, trailing off.

"I know," Robbie said. "I think we could do it."

"But how do we make a whole train of smokes just disappear?" Bert asked. "Are we going to pretend to be robbed or hijacked?"

They looked at each other for answers, but none came.

And that was fine with Bert.

He had trees on his mind.

CHAPTER SEVEN

"You almost got us killed!" yelled Fedora. "What the hell were you thinking!"

He rushed across the room, grabbed Jenkins by the collar and threw him on the floor.

Jenkins was not accustomed to physical activity, much less an assault, so he rolled to his side and stayed down, so shocked from Fedora's violence that he couldn't identify what part of his body was in pain.

Fedora advanced toward Jenkins for another assault but Jenkins turned his back and raised his hand.

"Enough," he said sharply. "That's enough!"

Fedora paused, fists still clenched, ready to

make Jenkins pay for what he did, or actually, didn't do.

"He had a gun!" Fedora yelled, more agitated. "How could you not know that? I don't know how I'm still alive!"

Jenkins shifted gingerly into a sitting position. Fedora took another step closer.

"Whippin' my ass won't change anything," Jenkins said. "It might make you feel better and make me feel worse, but it certainly won't help us talk about what's next."

Fedora looked over at his sidekick as if that idiot could provide any guidance. All he did was shrug his shoulders.

Fedora loomed over Jenkins, fists at the ready.

"Ok, mister genius, tell us what you have in store," Fedora said.

These three had come together in a most unlikely way and now were in an uneasy business relationship that was lucrative but fragile.

Their alliance began on one of those dark nights before there was good communication between the cigarette company's trains and the railroad company when Bert and Robbie sometimes had to spend the night on the siding after missing the connection with that night's north-bound freight train.

Jenkins had worked for months to understand where the missing cigarettes were going, how they were disappearing and who was behind it.

He hired detectives but they were useless. He rode the trains a couple of times with Bert and Robbie but nothing seemed amiss and the connections with the big freight trains had gone seamlessly.

Jenkins was desperate to understand how it worked. He analyzed the weak links of the train shipments and concluded the cigarettes were being stolen when they reached New York or Philadelphia. On two separate occasions he arranged for someone he trusted to meet the trains in those two cities when the trains arrived and open the boxcars as soon as the steel wheels stopped turning. On both trips, he opened the cars with a special key that worked special locks and discovered dozens of cases of cigarettes were already missing from each car.

It has to be here, thought Jenkins, as he crouched in the dark and frightening underbrush alongside the siding thirty miles from the factory flanked by two tough guys from the loading dock he commandeered to be his sidekicks, protectors and companions.

The train engineered by Bert that night was already parked at the siding, having missed the connection. Jenkins watched as Bert sat by a tiny fire and periodically clambered out of his chair to walk the length of the train with his flashlight and baton. The locomotive had gone cold; Bert would fire the boiler shortly before it was time to return to the factory.

The night was terrifyingly quiet except for the gnats buzzing in his ears. Jenkins concluded he was not cut out for this kind of work. He imagined all sorts of snakes and bugs crawling up his pant legs.

But, he thought, *it will be worth it if I can figure out how this works.*

Because I want it to work for me.

Off in the distance, Jenkins heard the whistle of the nightly north-bound passenger train and in moments it rushed by overwhelming the night with its blinding headlight, its speed and deafening sound.

The train sped away and silence returned to the underbrush.

Then Jenkins saw the swinging beam of a flashlight. It wasn't Bert's.

He squinted in the darkness but saw nothing but the swinging light.

He nudged his companions who looked at him waiting for the signal to spring out of their hiding place and inflict pain and justice.

Jenkins placed a hand on each of their forearms to signal them to stay still.

Two figures with one flashlight moved towards Bert's fire.

Bert didn't seem surprised to see them. Instead, he got up from his chair and walked with them toward the boxcar at the end of his train.

Jenkins was intrigued at what he saw next.

Bert unlocked that boxcar and the next two also and slid open their big doors.

Then came the sound of a truck cranking up only a few hundred feet from where Jenkins hid in the underbrush with the bugs and snakes.

The truck emerged from its own hiding place, headlights off, tires crunching on the rocks that supported the railbed of the sidetrack. The two men with the flashlight moved quickly, transferring several dozen cases of cigarettes into the bed of the truck then covering them with a tarp which one of them tied down while the other handed something to Bert. Jenkins figured that was the money.

To the great frustration of the tough guys, Jenkins decided on the fly that they wouldn't rush Bert and the thieves. He could deal with Bert anytime he wished; he wanted to know where these cigarettes were heading.

He tapped his companions on the shoulder and motioned for them to follow him.

They crept through the dark underbrush as quietly as they could and arrived at a car parked on a sideroad just as the truck passed by, its lights still out.

"That's them! Let's go!" Jenkins shouted at the car's driver, a famed local bootlegger who owned a highly modified and very fast Ford roadster which he had rented, along with the driver, to Jenkins for the evening. He cranked the unmuffled, eight-cylinder beast.

On most nights, the bootlegger ran from revenuers in this car which had fake, untraceable license plates just in case the good guys ever got close enough to him, which they never did. On this night he sent word to his law enforcement buddies that he would be chasing thieves, not running whiskey, so leave him alone.

Jenkins held tight. He'd never been in a car this powerful or this noisy. It was terrifying and exhilarating.

They sped down the two-lane road, headlights blazing, engine roaring, the bootlegger shifting smoothly through the manual gears like an artist.

As they rounded a curve they spotted the truck, moving much slower than them.

The bootlegger had an arsenal on board and he had told Jenkins ahead of time to use whatever he needed. Jenkins had already paid him well, so the bootlegger was happy to provide the service.

One of the tough guys lifted a shotgun from the floorboard of the backseat preparing to blast the rear tires of the truck, the backup plan if it looked like the thieves might get away.

As he lifted it, his finger touched the shotgun's hair trigger. An eardrum-shattering sound erupted in the car and buckshot exploded from the right barrel ripping through the thigh muscle of the colleague sitting next to him and carrying the blood and tissue of his friend's leg through a fist-sized hole in the side of the car and out into the night.

Jenkins whipped around at the shocking sound of the gunshot and stared in horror at the injured man writhing in the backseat, shrieking in pain as the shock of his injury hit his brain.

The bootlegger looked over his shoulder in disgust. Blood was splattered everywhere and there was a hole in the side of his beloved car.

He looked at Jenkins and lifted his hands, silently asking *What now?*

"Keep going!" Jenkins yelled at him, pointing at the truck. "Stick to the plan."

The bootlegger used the easy power of the car to pull alongside the plodding truck and the tough guy this time pointed the shotgun at the left rear tires of the truck and blew them both out.

The truck weaved back and forth as the back tires disintegrated and the driver wrestled the big steering wheel to stay in control. When he lost control, the truck ran off the side of the road where its good rear tires hit a culvert, and rolled onto its side.

The bootlegger slammed on the roadster's oversized brakes and stopped in the middle of the road, its headlights illuminating the wrecked truck, front wheels still spinning in the air.

The bootlegger jumped out of the car with

Jenkins and the uninjured tough guy. They all carried firearms as they surrounded the truck's cab to see if anyone was able to crawl from the wreckage.

"C'mon out!" Jenkins yelled. "We're not the law. You're not going to jail but I need to see some hands if you wanna live!"

Jenkins was momentarily shocked at the words flowing from his mouth. *Where did I learn to yell like this?*

The bootlegger cocked his forty-four-caliber hand gun which was so heavy he could barely lift it, but he believed in always having the biggest gun in a fight, even a knife fight. He pointed it at the windshield.

After a minute, a voice came from inside the truck. "Ok, ok, we're coming out. We don't have any guns. Don't shoot us!"

The truck rested on its right side so the heavy driver's door was finally pushed open. Fedora and his sidekick crawled out and toppled to the road beside their wrecked truck and into the headlights that blinded them.

A few hours later Jenkins had everything he needed.

Fedora was tied to a post in a little room at the

loading dock of the cigarette factory and explained it all to him, especially after his right index finger was jammed into the socket of a table lamp and the switch flipped on. His sidekick remained silent, eyes open in shock and fear.

The plan wasn't all that complicated, to Jenkins' surprise, but very clever and lucrative.

"And, now, my friend," Jenkins said, leaning in so he was inches from Fedora's face, "we're partners, for better or worse.

"You steal what I tell you and when I tell you and deliver where I tell you," he snarled at Fedora.

Fedora nodded at the sidekick who looked back in terror.

"Him too," Jenkins said.

"Got it," said Fedora. "Just tell us what you want."

CHAPTER EIGHT

Bert had never been this nervous when he had his hand on the old locomotive's throttle.

Sure, there had been times when a deer or cow would wander onto the tracks, but they were no match for the locomotive's tons of steel and coal and steam. He'd never hit anything at a crossing because traffic in these woods was mostly farmers and even they were rare.

Before today, Bert had never done anything bad except collect some cash when a few cigarettes were stolen from his train. He always thought it wasn't really bad unless somebody got hurt and nobody was getting hurt from a few pilfered cases of cigarettes.

And nobody was going to get hurt today.

Bert had always been loyal and reliable. He happily took his train from Durham three times a week pulling boxcars loaded with cigarettes down to the main line and returning to the tobacco factory with empty cars. The improvement he and Robbie had suggested to the cigarette company for each of them to operate a locomotive separately was working smoothly.

Today was Robbie's turn to make the trip and he was in Durham waiting for the boxcars to be loaded with their cargo.

Bert, meanwhile, was at the controls of his steam engine pulling five empty and stolen log cars up the easy grade toward a tree farm in rural Durham County instead of his usual load of empty cars back to the cigarette factory.

He had kept an eye on the log cars for months. They were parked on a siding down in Lee County and seemed to have been forgotten. He borrowed five today.

They were mostly rusted out junk, but they would serve his needs. He could tell from the noise behind him that several of the steel wheels on the cars had locked up or broken, the metal-on-metal shrieking like an alarm to everyone in the county.

John Millard's farm was in the middle of nowhere. He inherited a hundred acres of pine forest from his daddy. As soon as Daddy died and the will was settled, Millard's plan was to cut down the trees, grab the cash and get out of Durham.

He'd done the math and realized that sending the logs by truck to the pulp mill in Moncure would eat dramatically into his margins. A section of his farm touched the railroad right of way and he had talked to the owners of the textile mill about hauling his logs since they owned the railroad but their price ruined Millard's economics.

Then, one day, he was standing at the corner of his property pondering what to do when Bert came by spewing steam and coal smoke.

Millard found Bert later that week lying on his back under his locomotive trying to coax some grease into a mostly destroyed bearing on one of the drive wheels. They made their deal and today Bert was taking the cigarette factory's old locomotive and some stolen log cars to John Millard's farm.

Bert wasn't about to cut Robbie in on the deal. While Robbie was in Durham, Bert's plan was to pull the log cars to John's farm, get the logs loaded and then back down to New Hill and on to the pulp mill in Moncure. If all went according to plan he'd be out of the way when Robbie came from Durham and the stolen log cars would be safely back on their siding in Lee County. And a few thousand bucks would be in his pocket. *That'll make Eileen happy*.

He didn't exactly know how long it would take to load the logs but he had made Millard promise to have the logs piled by the rails and enough equipment to load them as quickly as possible. The last thing he needed was Robbie rounding the curve at thirty miles an hour and finding a bunch of log cars in his way.

But the more he thought about it, Bert realized he needed more time.

He found his solution one evening in the bar at the Jack Tar Hotel, which was not a typical place for Bert to be. But on this evening, he had some business to handle.

As he nursed a beer, two men came to the bar. They stood on either side of Bert, and pressed against him.

He looked at one, and then the other and did a double-take. They looked the same.

It was the twins.

Bert had heard about these twins. The word around town was they were truly worthless, small-time criminals who pretended to be big-time pimps and players. But he also heard they would do just about anything for money and were fairly reliable to be small-time crooks.

The bartender at the Jack Tar was their front man. He would contact them and set a meeting for a hundred bucks.

"I'm Roger," said the twin on the left, not looking at Bert or shaking his hand.

"And I'm Stanley," said the other one. "Whatcha want?"

Bert was heading into dangerous territory, and he almost had second thoughts now that he was at the bar with these guys. But he was in too far now.

"I need to buy some time," he said, staring at his beer glass.

The twins leaned forward and looked past Bert to look at each other, shrugging their shoulders.

"Do you know your way around the cigarette factory?" Bert asked.

The twins nodded yes.

"Well," Bert continued, "I need something to happen there that will slow down or stop the factory for a couple of hours. I need something that will delay a trainload of cigarettes from leaving the factory."

"Like what?" Stanley asked.

Bert replied, "I don't really care what it is, just some disturbance that screws up the manufacturing or shipping for a couple of hours."

"What do you want us to do?" Roger asked.

"How about I leave that up to you?" Bert said. "I'll pay you to buy me a couple of hours. How you do it is up to you. Create a disturbance, break a piece of equipment. I hear you guys are clever."

"Well, sure" Roger said. "If the price is right."

Bert made his offer, which was eagerly accepted. Half the money now, half when the job was done. He gave them a piece of paper with the date of the job.

And now that day had come.

Bert was on his way to the tree farm at midday. His nerves grew more frayed each time the locomotive's steel wheels hit a joint in the rails. It was only twelve miles but it seemed like a hundred and he was sure he'd see Robbie or his boss at every crossing wondering where Bert was going with his train and someone else's clanking log cars.

Finally, Bert saw John Millard in the distance standing on the track, hands on his hips. As Bert slowed, he could see logs stacked by the tracks and two contraptions he'd never seen before. One was belching steam and looked like a prehistoric monster with a big claw. The other was a primitive crane with lots of cable and pulleys and two hitched horses to provide the power.

Bert climbed down from the locomotive, pulled his conductor's watch and told Millard he had maybe five hours before Robbie came through on his way to the main line. *Get to work.*

Loading the first two cars went smoothly. The primitive crane started to load car number three while the steam machine started on number four. Suddenly there was a screech of twisting metal and a violent whizzing of cables suddenly freed from their burden and the banging of pulleys against the side of the railcar.

Parts of the crane flew in every direction as it toppled onto the locomotive. Logs tumbled into the ditch next to the rails and onto the rails themselves. The horses were startled by the cacophony as their leather harnesses came loose and they fled.

Bert stared in disbelief at the calamity.

Huge logs lay against one of the boxcars. Several had hit the rails. It even looked like one section had been knocked out of line. His locomotive continued to hiss and pant impatiently as if offended by the junk that had fallen on it. Millard held his hands in his head as he stared at his broken crane and watched his panicked horses run away. Bert looked at the remaining empty cars and knew there was nothing the twins could do in Durham that would give him enough time to save this job.

Then, in the distance, in the night, a train whistle.

Faint, miles away.

Bert listened, and turned his head. *Impossible! This is way too early for Robbie!* They were too far from the main line so it couldn't be one of those trains.

Bert listened.

Then, again, the whistle.

Louder this time.

Definitely a steam locomotive. He usually

loved listening to its unique sound but today it sounded threatening.

Bert was puzzled. The whistle would blow several times, then stop. Not the usual long-long-short-long blast at crossings. He couldn't make sense of it.

He turned violently to Millard. "I've got to get this train out of here! Do something with these logs! And help me get this shit off my locomotive!"

Three long whistle blasts, closer still.

Millard stood like he was drugged.

The train whistle, again. A long blast.

Bert quickly climbed into the cockpit of his locomotive and frantically shoveled coal to get the old machine ready to move. He threw the drive lever into reverse, and looked at the chaos on the tracks.

He pushed the throttle wide open. The big drive wheels spun wildly on the rails, and the train crept backwards.

The doomed crane and broken cable fell away from the engine as it started to move. Bert watched in dismay as a log became wedged between the undercarriage of one of the log cars and the crossties in the railbed. The old locomotive pushed hard, its drive wheels spinning, but the train stopped moving.

Suddenly the log dislodged a crosstie and the train lunged forward. Bert watched in horror as the log cars lurched on uneven rails but stayed on the tracks as the train picked up speed, and Bert held on.

Bert was underway. He pulled the throttle to reduce speed. As he did, the bolt holding the throttle to the control box sheared off and suddenly he held a throttle that was connected to nothing.

As he panicked, he looked over his shoulder at the mess he'd left behind. He saw in the distance the bright headlight of Robbie's engine. He could tell it was moving quickly. Too quickly. Maybe even as fast as fifty miles per hour, almost twice the speed he and Robbie ever moved.

Bert had no control over the speed of his locomotive now so he could do nothing to get out of the way of Robbie's speeding train. He was shocked by what he saw next.

Robbie's locomotive hit the damaged track, its headlight suddenly veering off.

The old locomotive took a violent turn toward the logs and steam crane next to the track. Rails came loose and flew through the air like spears. The locomotive rolled onto its side, spewing steam, dirt flying, its big drive wheels still spinning trying to stay alive. Then it was still. The boxcars tried to keep going straight but left the tracks also, some in the ditch, others mangled or jackknifed on the track.

Without a throttle, all Bert could do was throw on his brakes and hope the train clamored to a stop. It did. He jumped from the cockpit and ran down the railbed to the wreck to help Robbie. If he could be helped.

The wrecked locomotive hissed with anger as its boiler spilled steaming water and a small fire burned in the ditch where hot coals had been flung from the engine.

He spotted Robbie lying face down in the ditch very still, one leg twisted at an odd angle, a piece of rail across his back. He wrestled away the rail, and rolled Robbie so that he was lying on his back.

But it wasn't Robbie.

It was Roger!

He checked his pulse. Nothing.

He looked around for Robbie.

The cab of the derailed locomotive was empty.

He ran to the other side of the mangled tracks looking frantically for Robbie. He called out for him but realized the noise of the dying locomotive made that pointless.

Then he saw something under the first boxcar, lying on its side, with cartons of Chesterfields spilling on the tracks. It was a bloody hand. Bert rushed over and took the arm, and pulled. The arm came but without a body.

Bert recoiled in shock.

He peered under the debris, and pushed some of it away so he could get a better look at the armless body, which was face down. He rolled it over. It wasn't Robbie, either.

This is impossible!

He looked closer. It looked just like the body in the ditch!

Stanley!

How can this be?

Bert's head was spinning. Nothing made sense. The scene was a disaster with logs and rails and wrecked train parts, cigarette cartons strewn and the dead bodies of Roger and Stanley sprawled awkwardly amidst the chaos.

And he had caused it. Only one thing to do now.

He slowly walked back to his panting locomotive which waited patiently, coal smoke curling from its stack, steam escaping its valves.

He climbed into the cab using a pair of large pliers to ease open the broken throttle on the old locomotive.

He had five log cars in front of him since he was backing the train back towards New Hill. He couldn't really see beyond that as he moved out of Durham County and towards Chatham County and a very uncertain future. He hoped there wasn't any traffic on the rural roads that crossed the tracks but he sounded the whistle anyway and hoped to avoid another wreck.

At first, he didn't see Robbie standing at the Olive Chapel Road crossing frantically waving his arms. As the locomotive made the crossing Bert spotted him and threw the brakes.

Before he could completely stop, Bert jumped from the locomotive and ran toward Robbie.

"I got hijacked!" Robbie yelled, his eyes wide with panic. He looked back up the track. "Where's my train? They took my train! They're on their way! I got a car and tried to outrun them! Where are they?"

Robbie caught his breath and looked around. At the log cars.

"What are you doing?" he shouted at Bert. "Why are you on the railroad? What's going on?"

Bert looked at the confused Robbie, and drew a deep breath.

"I've done a terrible thing," he shouted to Robbie over the panting and hissing of the locomotive.

"There isn't time to explain. But here's the deal. If you want in on this, you have to decide right now and get on this locomotive with me. If you don't, turn and walk away and do what you have to."

Robbie hesitated.

Bert scrambled up the ladder into the cab of the locomotive and extended a hand to pull Robbie in after him.

Robbie refused the hand but instead stood frozen on the rocks of the railbed.

"I don't understand any of this!" he shouted at Bert.

Bert took a deep sigh, and moved the locomotive's rigged up throttle ahead just slightly. The machine hissed and spewed steam and jerked into motion.

"Get in, you idiot," he yelled at Robbie, "we're gonna get rich."

Robbie looked for a moment like he didn't know what to do. He looked down the tracks, and then up the tracks as if he was deciding which way to go.

Then he jogged toward the locomotive and grabbed the bottom rung of the ladder.

Bert helped him the rest of the way.

CHAPTER NINE

Bert and Eileen didn't have a car yet, so Bert walked back and forth to work.

It was just a couple of miles and the only bad part was when it was snowing or raining. He had his eye on his neighbor's white Rambler station wagon with a For Sale sign on the window and he'd been calculating whether they could afford it.

Robbie had the engineer duty and Bert was back at the maintenance shack taking care of details when he ran out of chores. They didn't punch a clock because they were now on salary so Bert changed out of his work clothes and began the two-mile walk home a little earlier than usual.

His route took him through a fading three-block business district that served mainly the folks who worked at the cotton mill. He didn't slow or browse, anxious to get home to Eileen. He continued down a boulevard lined with magnificent oak trees planted a generation ago to line the road to the long-forgotten clubhouse of the local public golf course.

He turned the corner at the little park across the street from his house which was three houses down from the tree-lined boulevard.

What he saw made him stop.

A car was in his driveway. There were never cars in his driveway. But there it was: a brown Chevrolet, late model, two-door.

His mind raced. He and Eileen didn't have any friends. No preacher would visit since they didn't go to church.

I'm a little early, could I have caught Eileen with a boyfriend?

That thought spurred him into a rapid walk cutting across the yard rather than using the sidewalk in his rush to get inside his home.

He threw aside the screen door and pushed open the front door but saw nothing. He looked left into the living room and quickly right into the unfurnished dining room. He couldn't imagine what he'd find in the bedroom.

He moved quickly down the narrow hallway to the back of the house.

He froze in a panic at what he saw.

Eileen was at their kitchen table dressed better than he'd ever seen her. He realized she was actually pretty when she wore the right clothes and makeup.

She was grinning at him.

And sitting on the lap of the man in the fedora hat.

His arm was draped over her shoulder, his right hand lazily dangling close to her breast. A cigarette hung loosely from his lips, its ashes littering Bert's kitchen floor.

"What the hell!" Bert yelled, glancing around his kitchen for some kind of weapon. He didn't own a gun or a baseball bat and the kitchen knives were too far away.

"Calm down," Fedora said, "I'm not gonna hurt her. In fact, we're delighted you're home early. She's getting heavy."

Eileen turned smiling toward Fedora and kissed him, once on the cheek and then on the lips.

"What ...?" Bert stammered, unable to even form a complete sentence. "Turn her loose!"

He started to rush toward Fedora, fists balled, desperate to assault this criminal.

Just then, the toilet flushed and from the couple's tiny bathroom emerged Fedora's colleague zipping his pants and wiping his hands on them. He pulled out a kitchen chair to block Bert's attack, turned it backwards and sat, his arms draped over the chair's back.

Eileen squirmed in Fedora's lap, wiggling her butt closer to him. Fedora dropped his hand, casually brushing it against her breast and looking at Bert to see if he'd react. Eileen smiled at her lover then turned to Bert.

"This is *my* man now," she said, sounding like a schoolgirl.

"I'm with *him* now," she reiterated, looking back at Fedora.

Fedora looked back at her, moved his hand slightly away from her breast and wondered how his brilliant plan had gone so badly wrong.

He hatched it after he and his buddy concluded they were probably stealing as many cigarettes as they could on a regular basis and someone was going to catch on eventually.

They needed one more big profitable job and then they could move away from minor-league cigarette thievery and onto an opportunity that was beginning to emerge, trafficking a new obsession among college kids who were addicted to a drug called marijuana. They knew little about it but it sounded like they could make a lot of money.

"You think they'll go for it?" Fedora's buddy had asked on the night their scheme was birthed in a beer bar a few miles from their usual cigarette-stealing rendezvous spot. "I mean, how do we know these cigarette guys won't turn on us?"

Fedora looked at his buddy like he had three heads.

"You idiot," he said, "these guys are in too deep. They've been paid thousands. They're bigger thieves than we are. Can't you see that? All we need is a foolproof way to keep them honest."

Fedora and his buddy initiated an audacious plan that had worked in the past.

Fedora's sidekick secretly shadowed Bert for a few days and followed him home from work a couple of times where he saw that his prey was greeted on the front porch of a small house by his wife.

He reported back to Fedora the little he'd observed. But the two of them decided that the best way to hold Bert's feet to the fire and keep him honest was through her.

For a crook, Fedora was a natural charmer, good-looking enough to get by and with enough personality to carry on a conversation that would hook any bored wife. His game was to innocently encounter the wife of his target, whether it was a banker or business owner or a poor sap Fedora was trying to rob or swindle, and cross her path at a public, neutral location, like the grocery or pharmacy.

He would charm her into trusting him and hold her hostage until her husband delivered the goods.

It always worked.

On a beautiful spring afternoon, Fedora made his move.

Eileen was sitting in the little city park across from the home she shared with Bert, glad the weather was nice enough to escape the house.

She was still wiping tears from a recurring sobbing jag she experienced when she felt like her life was stuck. Even though it was better than it ever had been, she felt like time was rushing by and she was missing opportunities.

She sat on a bench wistfully watching the young mothers herd their toddlers around the playground from the slide to the sandbox and then to the swing set.

She took a final, long drag on the unfiltered Camel dangling from the corner of her mouth, sucking the harsh smoke deep into her lungs before dropping the butt into a small coke bottle half-filled with water and the four other butts now soaked in a putrid mixture. When she left the park, she would drop the bottle into one of the park's trash cans.

This was a vice she picked up after moving here. She admitted to herself it was nasty. But it made her feel better. She had tried the brands made by her husband's company but none gave her the kick of the Camels with no filter to smooth them out. She loved the buzz even though most days she now had a raspy cough.

She was now up to a carton a week, always smoked at the park so there was no chance of Bert finding out. She bought her Camels on Bert's charge account at the Rexall drugstore and tipped the lady behind the counter a dollar to ring them up as cosmetics.

She lit another and snorted the smoke from the cigarette's glowing end into her nose just like she'd seen on tv.

"May I sit on this end?" came a soft voice, jarring her from her enjoyment. "I hope I'm not intruding."

Eileen turned toward the voice and saw a handsome man wearing a dark fedora, a rolled-up newspaper tucked under his left arm.

"Um, well," Eileen stuttered, a bit unsettled. "Sure, I guess."

Fedora smiled sweetly.

"I just want a quiet place to read my newspaper and those kids are making a lot of noise near the other benches," he said.

"Ok, sure," Eileen said, squirming toward the opposite end of the bench, tamping out her half-smoked Camel and dropping it into the Coke bottle where it made a soft and brief sizzling sound.

He sat and began flipping through the newspaper.

After a couple of awkward moments Eileen

pushed some loose hair out of her eyes and slowly got up.

"Please don't leave," Fedora said sadly. "I enjoy having you here, even if we don't talk or know each other. I just miss the company of a nice woman."

Eileen felt her face flush. She hadn't felt that in a long time.

"I enjoy our visits," she said. "I come here most days. We can visit anytime you like."

They shared brief times together on the bench over the next weeks as he worked his way into Eileen's life. She told him what he already knew about her husband's work and even hinted that she might be bored or unhappy, how small the house seemed at times. Fedora made up a preposterous story about a dead wife and a missing girlfriend and even managed to squeeze out a couple of crocodile tears as he recounted his sadness.

He certainly never expected Eileen to fall in love. The others never did.

But did she ever.

That had never happened before to Fedora with all the other wives because he typically scammed the witless husbands before things got so entangled.

But on a warm afternoon on the bench, she slid closer to him.

This may be my chance to escape this life, to do better than I've ever done, she told herself as she screwed up the courage.

She took his hand.

"I'm so sorry for all your losses," she said, trying to be sincere. "I can see you're hurting."

And then she looked into his eyes.

"Is there anything I can do?"

Fedora blinked back a couple of fake tears and momentarily felt guilty and concerned about heading into uncharted territory.

Before he could figure out his next step, Eileen figured out hers.

She stood, drawing him up from his place on the bench, his hand in hers.

Without speaking she led him across the sandy infield of the park's softball diamond, pausing briefly to drop the bottle into the trash can and then continued up the brick steps from the park toward the street.

She paused, looked at her house and back at

him as if to ask permission. She assumed no resistance was approval and crossed the street.

Together, hand in hand, they went up the steps of the little house and down the hall to the bedroom.

And now they were in the kitchen of this little house, just a few steps from that bedroom and just a few weeks away from what seemed like a good idea.

"We need to talk," Fedora said to an astonished and flabbergasted Bert. "Business."

"What business?" Bert said, his voice quivering with anger. "I'm not talking about anything until you let her go, or she lets you go, or something happens! This is insane!"

Fedora removed his arms from around Eileen who stopped smiling instantly. He shoved her roughly and awkwardly toward Bert who caught her.

She looked at him and then back at Fedora, hate in her eyes.

She knew immediately she'd been duped.

She was frightened and angry beyond imagination. She thought she might be sick.

She had just spent six weeks with Fedora. She was really in love and ready to escape with him to an exciting new life.

He was more handsome than Bert and a better lover even though any lover was better than Bert.

The man in the fedora had been kind and gentle and open about his feelings and his losses.

And, now he had shoved her back to her husband, back to reality.

"Bullshit," Eileen snarled angrily, glaring at Fedora. "You sonofabitch."

Bert whipped his head back and forth looking first at his wife trying to understand.

"Here's the deal," Fedora said.

Before he could continue, Eileen stormed to the kitchen counter, thrust her hand deep into a box of Cheerios and pulled out an already opened pack of Camels hidden inside. She pulled out a cigarette, tamped it down on the counter like she'd seen on tv and lit it with a kitchen match.

She took a couple of deep drags on the Camel, held her breath, then walked over to Fedora, just inches from his face, and blew a flume of caustic blue smoke in his face. He gasped, coughing as his eyes watered and throat burned.

Eileen then inhaled another lungful of Camel smoke, walked over to Bert and blew the smoke into his face.

Bert gasped as he tried to catch his breath. Fedora moved toward Eileen, arm raised to strike her across the face.

Then a figure appeared at the kitchen screen door, interrupting Fedora's assault.

With great flourish the person there tried to fling open the screen door but it was hooked from the inside like every good southern home. The person's shoulders sagged in defeat.

"Please unhook it," Jenkins said quietly to the group in the kitchen, "and let me in."

Fedora's sidekick flipped the hook. Jenkins regained his posture and strode into the room looking from one person to the next.

"You must be Eileen," he said, smiling when his eyes landed on her.

A windstorm of acrid, blue smoke erupted from her mouth and enveloped his head.

"Yes, you're Eileen," he said, blinking his burning eyes.

She then whipped around and walked toward

front of the house looking over her shoulder at the mob in her kitchen.

She paused, turned toward the group and locked eyes with Jenkins, a faint smile on her lips.

She stared deeply at him then swiveled around and strode from the room looking over her shoulder once more before moving through the doorway.

Jenkins followed every move as she walked away.

He continued to look at the doorway, now empty.

Then, hacking slightly, he spoke to the tiny group in the kitchen.

"Now, we have work to do."

CHAPTER TEN

Bert sat inside the Top Hat bar on Broad Street as he waited for Robbie to show up.

The inside of the bar smelled like a pizza you'd never want to eat but eating was the last thing on Bert's mind.

The dreadful smell mingled with that of stale beer and spilled onto the sidewalk through the front door, which, on warm days, was held open with a rope tied to a nearby downspout. Bert briefly wondered why anyone ever came to this dump.

But he had more important problems to consider.

He was still reeling from what happened in

his kitchen the previous day, the least of which was his suddenly a chain-smoking, cheating wife. Unfiltered Camels? Banging Fedora? But that would have to wait another day.

He was still trying to get his brain around the outlandish plan outlined by this man named Jenkins whom Bert had heard of around the cigarette factory and knew was a powerful man in the company but had never seen or met before yesterday.

Jenkins explained the plan to the small group assembled in the kitchen after Eileen went to the front porch.

He told everyone in the kitchen that they were all a part of the plan, that they would be richly rewarded and that snitching or bailing would result in the most severe of consequences. Bert noted that Fedora and his buddy seemed to understand the meaning of this threat more than Bert.

All he knew was that he was a key part of Jenkins' plan and that he couldn't say no or something bad would happen.

Bert was still mulling this over, sipping a beer that had grown warm from inattention when

Robbie walked in. He sniffed the air with a grimace then joined Bert at the bar.

"What's the matter?" Robbie asked.

"Man, I have no idea what's going on, but it's big and it's a mess," Bert said.

He took another sip of his warm beer while Robbie waited for a cold one.

"Okay, I can handle it," Robbie said.

Bert swore Robbie to secrecy then spent the next half hour sharing what he knew. At the end of the story, they both sat at the bar with their heads in their hands. The bartender had seen enough to keep away.

"I can't handle this," Robbie finally admitted quietly. "This messes up our plan. Hell, I'd already decided how to spend the money."

"It sure seems like it's messed us up," Bert said.

Bert thought wistfully of all the planning he and Robbie had done. They had proven they could operate their scheme without any interference from the cigarette company. They had to deliver the boxcars full of cigarettes to the main line as expected and those smokes (at least most of them) got where they were supposed to.

The big wreck at the tree farm, as bad as it

was, proved they could get away with it. Bert used a locomotive for something other than company business and had even illegally borrowed some unused log cars without getting caught.

A couple of big cranes were rented from the main line to put Robbie's old locomotive back on the tracks and the textile company that owned the tracks had to fix them because the cigarette company had a solid contract to use them.

All of this with no skin off their noses.

Bert and Robbie became emboldened.

Over the months, they studied the schedules of the main line railroad, its freight trains and its passenger trains. Robbie even stowed away in one of the cigarette boxcars after it was hooked up to a north-bound freighter and secretly rode it all the way through Philly and into New York to learn more about how the train was switched and sidetracked and maneuvered to its final destination at warehouses across the river from Manhattan.

They concluded that all of this was way too complicated and there was no way one of their locomotives could pull a train loaded with stolen cigarettes up the east coast without colliding with another train, being sidetracked and searched by the authorities, being switched by accident to the wrong city or being stranded on a spur line to a cement plant or some other godforsaken place.

They came up with a simpler plan.

When the madness had ensued in the kitchen the previous day, Bert and Robbie were just days away from implementing their plan.

But it was no longer their plan.

Our hijacking plan has been hijacked!

Their elbows rested on the sticky bar.

They read each other's minds.

Do we have a choice?

They looked at each other with no answer, and ultimately said their goodbyes.

As Robbie stepped on the sidewalk, he remembered how Bert left him out of the tree deal.

He stopped for a moment and thought, staring at the sidewalk and smelling the stale beer.

He knew what he had to do.

And he'd never felt more alone.

CHAPTER ELEVEN

Jenkins was surprised.

He always thought a meeting with the mob bosses who controlled some of the Jersey ports would be a more dignified affair perhaps at a country club with bottles of wine or at a fancy restaurant with an obsequious owner fawning over his menacing guests fearful of getting shot in the back of the head if the branzino wasn't served at the correct temperature.

This certainly was not any of those.

He had been brought to a pier located on a filthy, debris-strewn tributary of the Hudson River by a couple of goons stationed not so discretely near the front door. They had picked him up in a pre-arranged spot at Penn Station after observing him long enough to determine he wasn't being followed by the cops or their bosses' competitors.

After a circuitous journey through Manhattan and across the river into Jersey, Jenkins was brought to the derelict pier poking sadly into the tributary and delivered to the front door of a squat building. There were no cranes, forklifts or containers that he could see and certainly no ships docked nearby.

The building was actually two old shipping containers attached end-to-end so it was one long rectangle box that looked like a pair of mobile homes hitched together. The containers obviously had been at sea for many years because the interior where he joined the bosses smelled like a spoiled oyster. The bosses smelled like they had been swimming in an ocean of sewer water. Jenkins felt out of place in his clean suit.

The meeting had been arranged with the bosses by Fedora, who sold his stolen cigarettes to the underlings and minions of the two bosses sitting with Jenkins in the long box today. Like most in organized crime they kept their distance from the actual transactions that funded their empires. They knew few details and asked no questions as long as their guys delivered the right amount of money every week.

It had taken months to arrange the meeting as Fedora convinced the underlings it was safe and discreet and not some sort of FBI setup. There had been a lot of back-and-forth negotiations about where to meet and how to get there as the bosses and their associates took every precaution to ensure that this meeting with a stranger wasn't some sort of trap that would get them killed or imprisoned.

Meanwhile, Jenkins grew more impatient every week. He had stalled the old man's desire to meet with his phantom suppliers as long as he could. Time was running out and he needed to get this deal done.

He was patted down by one of the goons and motioned through the door into the dank box where he sat facing the two bosses.

There had been no handshakes, no pleasantries. Nobody offered him coffee or sought to exchange business cards.

They were seated across from one another at a folding picnic table, sitting in cheap yard chairs.

"So, where do we start?" asked Jenkins, breaking the thick silence.

The bosses just stared back and then looked at each other.

Finally, one of them spoke.

"How much can you deliver?" he asked.

"As you know," Jenkins said, a slight tremble in his voice, "this is a one-time deal but it's a big one."

He went on to describe an arrangement where, on a particular night, a north-bound freighter's regular boxcars would be unhooked and parked on a side track. Boxcars full of cigarettes would take their place and be hooked to the engines. His engineers would take over the operation of the train which would proceed up the east coast using the signals and operational plans for the original train.

The hijacked train would stop short of its intended destination in Newark and park on a siding at an abandoned warehouse in Perth Amboy. It would be up to the mobsters to supply the manpower and vehicles to unload the train.

"I already asked how much can you deliver?" the mobster repeated. "Don't waste my time making me ask again."

Jenkins cleared his throat, unsure of whether to explain the math about how many cases fit in a train car or how many cartons are in a case. As he looked into the dead eyes of these guys, he decided to go the bottom line.

"Seventy million," he said.

He looked back and forth at the two mobsters, looking for something but saw nothing.

"Say it again," demanded the mobster with a furrowed brow.

"Seventy million. Cigarettes. Seventy thousand cases," Jenkins said.

The two mobsters blinked and moved uncomfortably in their seats. One of them cleared his throat and scratched his head. Jenkins couldn't tell if his number was too high, or too low. Or if there was a different problem.

One of them pulled out a little notepad and nub of a pencil and started doing some math using his thick fingers to count. He wrote some numbers on the notepad and showed the results to the other, eyebrows raised. They turned their backs to Jenkins for a whispered conversation. This went on for several minutes until one of them turned to Jenkins.

"Step outside," he said in a low but threatening voice. Jenkins did what he was told.

The goons were waiting there but didn't look at him.

He could hear talking inside the metal box but it didn't sound like arguing or angry conversation. He waited.

Finally, a loud voice from inside.

"Get back in here."

He opened the door to the box with a trembling hand and returned to his seat trying to read the faces of the mobsters to see if they'd made a decision, and if he'd be kept alive.

"Can you live with this?" one of the bosses asked, pushing a slip of paper toward Jenkins.

Jenkins was astounded by the number.

It was three times what he expected.

He didn't flinch or react. He just sat, looking at the slip of paper.

They stared at him, then looked at each other, and then back at him.

"Ok, we didn't expect your number," one of the bosses said. "It's a lot bigger than we had planned so we have some transportation issues and we'll have to hire extra guys. That eats into our margins if you know what we mean."

Jenkins was an experienced negotiator but was reluctant to try to squeeze more out of an already unbelievable deal, especially with mob bosses.

"Okay, I understand," Jenkins said. "But the increased size of the load actually means bigger margins for you even if your overhead is more."

The bosses were in no mood for a lecture.

"Listen, man," the boss continued, "we've never done a deal this big. The cash isn't the problem, it's the logistics. Can you live with what we're talking about? Do you need to talk to your partners or anybody else?"

Jenkins waited another moment. He realized that he had the upper hand.

"Ok, we have a deal," he said.

He expected a handshake from the mobsters at the delivery of this news.

The mobsters continued to stare at him. He asked for their notepad.

He wrote down three things, one at a time.

First, a delivery date. One of them pulled out a little calendar book, looked at the notepad, and nodded.

Then Jenkins wrote down a large number.

"I need this before I leave town, as a down payment and to cover our expenses," he said.

The two bosses looked at the paper, then each other, and back at Jenkins, and nodded.

He wrote down another number, and pushed it toward them.

"This is the cash in my hands on the loading dock of the warehouse when you confirm the load is accurate," Jenkins said.

The mobsters quickly did the math, and nodded.

Then they both reached out, and took turns shaking Jenkins's hand, still not smiling.

CHAPTER TWELVE

This will never work.

That was one of a thousand thoughts crowding Jenkins' mind on the morning of the delivery.

He drove up by car through the night to be there when the train arrived ... if it arrived at all.

There was no power to the warehouse so it was dark except for the light from nearby streets and buildings that barely spilled onto the property. With all the creepy shadows, Jenkins actually wished there was no light at all.

On the coldest, dampest morning Jenkins had ever experienced he now stood in a driving sleet storm on the platform of an enormous abandoned warehouse in Perth Amboy where it was very possible that his life might end.

And nobody was here.

No trucks, no workers, no hoodlums and worst of all, no train.

All he could think of was the millions of things that could go wrong.

He had no idea whether the hijack had worked back in North Carolina. Which meant that he also had no idea if the train could maneuver through the myriad of switches up the east coast and avoid calamity along the way. The mob bosses assured him that they had the right people on their payroll who would throw the switches in Jersey to guide the train to the warehouse.

But, what about between North Carolina and Jersey? Who did those switches?

And was he even at the correct warehouse?

Where was everybody?

As he stood on the platform, dawn was still an hour away, so there was no sign of light yet in the eastern sky and flakes of snow had joined the sleet to make it more miserable.

He waited for something to happen, freezing and shivering in the Jersey winter.

He had no idea how serene his drive through the night to this awful place had been compared to the events at the other end of the rail line.

Bert and Robbie had done their jobs for the last two days, assembling boxcars at the factory and making sure they were fully loaded and locked for the trip to the main line.

Late in the afternoon they coupled Bert's locomotive to the train and began the slow, easy ride through the country toward the main line. The only interruption to a smooth trip was the area at Millard's old tree farm where the textile company had trusted the repairs to the lowest bidder who left the tracks uneven causing the train rock back and forth like a ship in a stormy sea.

When they arrived at the siding they waited nervously, the old locomotive panting as Bert fed her just enough coal to keep the boiler going. Every moment was agony as it became dark and they imagined every calamity that could befall them, wreck their plans and send them to prison.

But, as they sat on the tracks, nothing happened; no railroad cops, nobody from the cigarette factory, no nosy sheriff's deputy wanting to kill time visiting with the railroad guys.

Finally, they heard the Seaboard freighter's whistle in the distance. They looked at each other, anxiety and fear in their eyes.

The freighter approached as the afternoon turned to dusk.

As it hissed to a stop, Fedora did his job, storming the cab of the Seaboard engine, tying up and gagging the stunned and frightened engineer.

Fedora's helper was sent to handle the conductor in the caboose. He slowly climbed the iron steps on the rear of the caboose but lost his footing and fell onto the rocks next to the tracks, twisting his ankle, screaming in pain.

"Who's there?" shouted the angry conductor as he rushed out the backdoor of the caboose, railroad lantern in one hand, baton in the other. He waved the lantern back and forth trying to see into the dark.

A man writhed on the rocks, holding his ankle.

"Who are you, you trespassing SOB?" the conductor shouted angrily. "I'll teach you to mess with the railroad!"

The conductor quickly came down the steps and attacked the helpless man, beating him on the head with his baton and nearly setting him on fire when he swung his lantern and doused the idiot with its kerosene.

If the conductor had been less focused on beating the hell out of Fedora's man and more on escaping he could've gotten away. But while he was beating up the guy, Robbie rushed to the ruckus and hit the conductor with a wrench, dropping him on top of his hapless victim. Robbie pulled him off, tied him up, and hauled him back into the caboose.

Fedora then appeared, slapped his helper in the face, helped him to his feet, and they both vanished into the evening.

Bert and Robbie then began the process of moving railcars back and forth, pushing the train's regular cars onto the sidetrack and replacing them with the ones loaded with cigarettes they had brought from the factory.

In the cockpit, Bert marveled that the controls of the freighter's diesel electric engine were much simpler to operate than the steam locomotive, which required more magic than engineering to make it operate properly with lots of levers to constantly pull this way and that and temperatures to monitor to keep the boiler from blowing to smithereens.

Meanwhile, at the other end of the long train Robbie thought about what would happen next for a long time, during sleepless nights and restless days.

Will I have the courage?

Ever since the incident at Millard's tree farm Robbie never fully trusted Bert. He never understood why Bert thought he could pull off an operation like that tree deal without Robbie finding out. And Robbie was never completely comfortable about the heist that was now underway.

What if Bert cuts me out of the payoff? What if Jenkins cuts us both out?

What if something worse happens?

Robbie thought about it constantly, unsure in his heart and mind what he should do.

And now it was time to either act with courage or accept that his fate, and perhaps his life, was in the hands of others.

Robbie was wrestling with his emotions and a potentially life-altering moment when that opportunity came.

Off in the distance he heard a single toot, the signal that the hijacked train was ready to move.

As Bert smoothly set the throttle on the

freighter and it began to crawl forward, Robbie threw the lock on the coupling that connected the last ten cars and caboose to the rest of the train.

The train began to move more quickly. Robbie heard the boxcars' couplings banging and clanking and their wheels squawking.

Bert was a half mile away in the cab of a long train and had no way of knowing that he was pulling ten cars fewer than planned.

His train headed north and picked up speed.

Robbie's cars remained where they were.

His moment had come.

There was no turning back.

CHAPTER THIRTEEN

The sleet and flurries turned to snow, increasing the suffering Jenkins was already enduring at one of the most miserable places he'd ever been.

The mob bosses added to his agony by finally showing up to check things out then sent a signal that resulted in trucks and men gathering on the loading dock. The bosses raised their hands in disgust when they saw the empty tracks and looked at their gold Rolexes impatiently.

Everyone was waiting for Jenkins' train.

He had no idea where it was and there was no way to contact Bert to find out whether it was even on its way or had been switched to

Pennsylvania or Timbuctoo or confiscated by the FBI.

"What's the deal?" asked one of the bosses.

"It'll be here," Jenkins replied, hiding his uncertainty.

"Let's step inside," the boss said with a nod of his head to Jenkins who followed him and the other boss out of the snow and into the frigid warehouse.

"We don't know what kind of crap you're pulling but we're burning through a stack of cash out there with those guys and the trucks and all you can say is 'it'll be here'?" The boss leaned his face toward Jenkins'.

"Honestly, I'm not pulling any crap," Jenkins tried to assure him, a nervous twitch pulsing on his face. "And to show my good faith, I have your up-front money in my car. I'll give it back if something has happened to the train."

The bosses looked at each other and appeared to relax. Jenkins didn't know what else to say so he remained quiet.

An hour passed uncomfortably. Then another even more so.

Jenkins was starting to panic about the train but was more worried that these goons and their employees might think it was a good idea to throw him in the sewage-filled ditch behind the warehouse with a bullet in the back of his head than to wait much longer for a train that might not come.

The snow didn't stick to the ground before it turned into a cold rain and everyone sought cover in the warehouse.

The mob bosses looked at Jenkins like lions at a wildebeest just before feasting.

Then, in the distance, a train whistle.

Three long toots, one short one.

The signal.

"That's him!" shouted Jenkins, thankful he might be allowed to keep his life.

The bosses looked at their Rolexes and shrugged their shoulders.

The train noisily moved down the tracks toward the warehouse, headlights flashing on and off, bell ringing.

Bert leaned his body out the window of the cab waving and grinning.

He stopped the engine just past the end of the loading dock so the first group of boxcars were accessible from the dock, and climbed down from the train, its engine still idling.

"Thank god," Jenkins said to him with relief, then asked, "is everything alright?"

"It is now," Bert said with a big smile.

"I want to hear about it later but we've got to get going," Jenkins said.

With that, he motioned to the bosses to follow him. He went to the first boxcar, pulled a big key from his pocket and slid it into the massive lock on the sliding door of the car. He threw the latch and slid open the door.

The car was neatly packed with a thousand cases of Chesterfields.

Jenkins looked at the bosses, smiling. They looked back at him with dead eyes.

They repeated the process with the next three cars. At each car, Jenkins slid open the door, and there were another thousand cases.

They skipped to the tenth car, another thousand cases.

The bosses kept their end of the deal.

After the tenth car was opened and a thousand cases was confirmed, one of them thumbed to a junior goon, who moved to the rear of one of the trucks.

Oh no, this is where they keep the machine gun.

Instead of a flurry of bullets, the junior goon unloaded eight suitcases onto the loading dock, and opened one of them, motioning Jenkins to come over to inspect.

It was full of cash. He assumed the others were also and wasn't going to risk insulting the bosses or their people by insisting on a full counting.

He rolled the suitcases two at a time to his car, barely large enough to hold them all.

He made them fit.

Then he thought about his situation.

He had his cash.

The mob had their smokes.

Why did he need to stick around while they unloaded the train?

What if they got what they wanted and decided to keep Jenkins's money also?

These guys were mobsters. He assumed there was honor amongst them, but he was an unknown outsider. Mobster courtesies probably wouldn't be extended to him.

What if he hung around only to end up in that sewage ditch with a bloody hole in his head? Why exactly did he still need to be here?

He looked around.

He was on the other side of the warehouse in the parking lot and out of sight of all the mobsters efficiently unloading the cases into the trucks.

Jenkins went to his car, crammed full of suitcases.

He could be out of here in a few seconds and quickly swallowed up by the morning rush hour traffic in Perth Amboy.

They'd never find him. They had no idea where to look.

When they realized he was gone, would they hold Bert hostage? Kill him?

Jenkins decided he couldn't worry about that. Collateral damage.

He surveyed the scene a final time. Nobody could see him.

He started the car.

It was the smartest move of his life.

A moment after he roared out of the parking lot, one of the junior minions reported to the bosses that some of the cars were missing.

CHAPTER FOURTEEN

This was the longest night of Robbie's life.

After he had uncoupled the ten cars from the rest of Bert's northbound train, he moved the caboose and its unhappy prisoner back to the end of the train of cars that had originally been destined for New York. Bert and Robbie never really had a plan for what would happen to those cars; they figured Seaboard would eventually find them, haul them to their destination and search for the thieves.

He then began the long and tedious journey through the darkness of rural North Carolina using the rails of short line and regional railroads, hardly a straight line between two points as he avoided the main lines and their fast-moving freight and passenger trains. He had worked out secret agreements with the short lines to reserve time and space on their tracks. It cost some money but the return on the investment would be worth it.

As the old locomotive chugged earnestly through the night filling its cab and engineer with dust and soot, Robbie became increasingly anxious about what he'd done and his betrayal of Bert. He hoped the nasty customers on the other end of the deal would be merciful to his friend.

As the miles passed, his anxiety eased and he became more comfortable in his decision that led to this trip.

He honestly didn't know if he would have been paid his share of the cigarettes headed north tonight. He was a small player in a big job. Who knew what would happen?

He backed his train along a rickety abandoned rail line to this isolated patch of Carolina foothills where he finally uncoupled his locomotive from the ten purloined boxcars.

Dawn would break in a few minutes and he was anxious to get this old locomotive out of the area before the local folks woke up and started pointing fingers at the unusual site of a steam engine on a set of tracks that hadn't been used in years.

The cigarettes he pulled to this hidden location would set him up for life. He didn't have a buyer but he would find one. And any price he charged would be a nearly a hundred percent profit for him because this part cost him almost nothing. It was like an insurance policy.

One of the hundreds of issues he had to solve was finding enough coal for this trip. The tender on the locomotive didn't have the capacity for the clandestine trip to the foothills and back so he arranged for an early morning rendezvous in a tiny community after he dropped off the boxcars.

One of the short lines agreed to help if the price was right. They negotiated an outrageous price for a dump truck full of lump coal to be standing by at the rail company's shops when Robbie came through the little town that was home to the short-line railroad company.

It was beginning to get light and Robbie and his locomotive were rolling about ten miles faster than allowed by the short line in order to make the coal rendezvous while it was still dark which had been a requirement of the short line for some reason.

Robbie slowed the locomotive as he approached the short line's shops where a trainman stood by to throw the switch that would send Robbie into the yard to pick up his coal.

As the big engine huffed into the yard, its huge headlight illuminated a sight that stopped Robbie's heart.

A dump truck was there along with a conveyor on the back of another truck to transfer the coal.

Flanking these two trucks were two other vehicles. As he moved closer their blue lights began flashing.

Robbie panicked.

There's no way to stop a locomotive, throw it in reverse and get the hell out of there. An ancient locomotive just doesn't work like that. It would be a helluva interesting chase but it wouldn't last long.

He peered into the scene in the headlight's glare and saw several people standing on the tracks. One was holding up his hand as if to tell Robbie to stop.

Robbie's mind raced. He had to think quickly.

Somebody ratted me out!

But who? Bert? He had no idea about Robbie's betrayal and was hundreds of miles from here. There's no way he could've figured it out and set this trap.

Robbie hadn't planned for any of this! He trusted these railroad guys to be cool about this deal and now the cops were waiting for him. There was no plan for this, no contingency at all.

He acted instinctively.

He slammed the throttle of the old locomotive wide open and she lurched forward, her drive wheels briefly spinning a half turn on the tracks, steaming and hissing and smoke pouring from her stack.

The people standing on the tracks hesitated briefly, not believing what they saw. The huge machine suddenly lunged forward and wasn't going to stop. They jumped to the side.

As the locomotive picked up speed Robbie had only seconds to decide what he must do.

He looked to his right and to his left.

He jumped out the right side.

As he landed on the rocks of the road bed, he simultaneously heard locomotive speed away and pick up speed and felt the sickening snap of the lower bone in his right leg.

He rolled over in pain on the rocks and looked up to watch the driverless locomotive keep moving.

One of the short-line guys realized what was happening and tried to jump on the train. But it was moving too fast and kept rolling faster and faster until it smashed into an antique and priceless passenger car that was parked outside the short line's shop while undergoing a million-dollar renovation.

The crash knocked the antique car sideways off the track, pushing it in the corner of the rail shop's wall. The locomotive came slightly off the rails enough to stop its progress and allow somebody to climb in the cab and kill the throttle.

Blinded by pain, Robbie couldn't move. He was quickly surrounded by people shining flashlights in his face.

They made a cursory glance at his mangled leg but did nothing to help him.

Instead, they made him stand, the pain almost more than he could tolerate.

"I've been looking for you," said one of the men, who led him not to a police vehicle but to a luxury car that smelled of rich leather.

CHAPTER FIFTEEN

Bert finally made it back from New Jersey after two awful days on buses that required him to make connections in Washington and Richmond.

He was lucky, and he knew it.

When the mob realized the train was ten cars short, it was a terrifying scene.

Guns were pulled out by nearly everyone. The bosses realized that Jenkins was gone and dispatched their minions to find him. They returned quickly, obviously without him, with the classic hands-in-the-air move that meant they didn't know where to start the search.

The bosses were embarrassed to be duped and

couldn't believe they were so reckless that they didn't count the cars but a sixty-car train looks a lot like a seventy-car train.

Then, they concluded that sixty thousand cases were still a lot of smokes and a lot of cash and a lot of profit so they returned their focus to getting them off this stolen train before somebody discovered where it was.

Bert was shocked when he realized the train was short. He panicked. He looked for Robbie who should've been in the caboose, except there was none. Bert couldn't even think. *What happened? How could this go so wrong? Where's Robbie?"*

The news of the missing cars caused all hell to break out on the loading dock. There was no time to search for Robbie. Bert couldn't understand what had happened, but he knew it was time for him to vanish.

He took advantage of the chaotic scene to sprint around the end of the warehouse, crawl through a hole in the fence and disappear into the world of Perth Amboy.

It was early in the morning two days later when Bert finally stepped off the bus in Durham and began the long walk to his little house across the street from the park.

He was so tired he could barely function. He was confused about what happened with the train and he was panicked about Robbie's whereabouts. He was relieved that he got away from the mobsters.

He pushed the thoughts about Robbie's fate from his weary mind and focused on going home to learn if Eileen was still there. And, if she was there, to see if she had any explanation for her strange behavior.

As he walked, he admitted to himself that he had reconciled that she had been swindled by Fedora who used her for bait to make sure Bert cooperated with this complicated scheme that thankfully was moving toward a conclusion even with some major problems.

Honestly, he had mixed feelings. She'd done some truly rotten things but he was prepared to forgive her. As he walked down the oak-lined streets toward home, his jacket slung over his shoulder and his small tote bag held in one hand, he developed the speech he'd deliver to her as he prepared to forgive her and move on.

He turned the corner toward his house, and stopped.

There was a man he didn't recognize sitting at the top of the brick steps that led to his front porch.

What now?

He cut across the little front yard of his home and strode bravely to the steps, poking his chest out to look more intimidating than he really was.

"Can I help you?" he asked the man.

"No, you cannot," was the reply, delivered so coldly that it frightened Bert.

"Who are you? Why are you on my front porch?" Bert demanded. "Is Eileen here? Is this about her? Are you a friend of hers?"

The man looked at Bert squarely in the eyes for a moment without speaking or blinking.

Then he said:

"I've been looking for you."

CHAPTER SIXTEEN

So, this is what it's like to be kidnapped.

At first, Jenkins was disoriented, a rag blindfolding his eyes and bitter-tasting tape gagging his mouth. He may have been unconscious for a few moments after being smacked in the head during the attack.

His head hurt, and when he tried to move his arms he realized he was tied down probably to the arms of the chair. His legs were also tied to the chair apparently, since he couldn't move them either.

His nose was unencumbered and he thought, *I'm lucky I don't have a head cold or I'd smother to death.*

Nothing covered his ears. He listened carefully but there was nothing to hear.

What is that smell? he asked himself over and over in the darkness and silence. It was vaguely familiar. He wiggled enough that his nose finally rubbed against something.

Burlap.

He smiled beneath the tape that irritated his parched lips, pleased he had solved the riddle. He couldn't see so he surmised that his captors had draped his head in a burlap sack.

He was actually unconcerned. He knew that his captors probably only wanted money so he was probably safe from some sort of physical harm. If they wanted him dead, he'd be dead already.

So, he sat quietly waiting for the inevitable removal of his hood and the presentation of a list of demands from the criminals who had done this to him.

This is not a kidnapping. This is a total betrayal by a bunch of lightweight criminals.

He was angry at what had happened, frustrated he hadn't seen it coming and that he had trusted these lowlifes. And, even though he was in bed and in business with the lowlifes, he never for a moment thought of himself as a criminal. *I'm a businessman plain and simple, not one of them.*

It had to be Fedora and his helper doing this for whoever they worked for. But they were too stupid to do this on their own. They were working for someone.

He thought about it for a minute.

Could it be the mobsters? The Jersey mob most certainly was looking for him and probably wanted him dead. He surmised that he would already be dead if this attack had been orchestrated by them. If it was like the movies, he would never know he'd been whacked. Someone would find his body face down with a bullet hole in the back of his head and his face blown off.

No, it wasn't the mob, but it was someone as powerful.

It happened as he walked home through the parking lot of the cigarette factory on the sidewalk that sliced through the parking lot filled with worn-out sedans and eventually crossed the railroad tracks that divided the town – the factories, poor people and workers on one side, everyone else on the other.

His house was a mansion by most standards and stood in a line of similar mansions that stretched for two blocks along the railroad, where the bigwigs at the factory lived. They all looked like southern plantation houses with huge columns on expansive front porches, perfectly manicured yards maintained by the lowest, most un-trained workers at the factory whose jobs included the yard work.

Trains woke everyone in the mansions in the dark of night. When the sun rose, the view out the front of their windows was the factory they ran, never out of sight, never out of mind. In years to come the successors to him and his colleagues would live out in the country at golf clubs and gentleman farms and commute to work in luxury cars.

But, today, he simply had to cross the tracks, his linen suit coat draped over his right shoulder, his worn, brown leather attaché held lightly in his left hand.

He was mildly melancholy because this was likely the final walk to his mansion by the tracks.

The events of recent days meant his world had changed and he could no longer be here.

No train was in sight or due for hours but he nevertheless paused short of the rails out of habit and his natural conservative cautiousness, looked both ways and saw nothing out of the ordinary, including what was sneaking up behind him.

A hood was thrown over Jenkins's head and his hands quickly tied. There was a blow to his head, and he was briefly dizzy and maybe passed out for a moment.

The rest was a blur.

As his brain started to clear, he sat bound, blinded and with a headache. He wondered what a steady dose of sucking air through a burlap bag would do to his brain while developing a plan to assemble whatever money would be demanded and any trickery he could use to deliver less than demanded and still escape alive.

Without warning there was a sudden jerk in his dark world, almost enough to topple his chair.

Then he heard the familiar sounds of a train getting underway, the banging and clanging of couplings between the railcars slamming back and forth against each other as they adjusted to the strain.

His chair swayed gently with the movement of the train and he swayed with it. The only sensation of speed was the increasing frequency of the clatter of steel wheels as they crossed the seams in the rails. He could hear an occasional distant whistle, probably from the locomotive of this train, but it seemed far away and he concluded that his location in the train was probably a long way from the front.

After a few minutes he concluded the train was moving rapidly based on the rhythmic clatter of the wheels. The swaying became more pronounced. The train was moving quickly and gaining speed.

Then, a sixth sense that someone was here.

The bile of panic rose in his throat. He tried to cry out but the bitter-tasting tape stifled his voice.

The burlap sack was slowly lifted from the right side of his head to expose his right ear.

Then, a voice in that ear, quiet enough to be menacing and terrifying but just loud enough to be heard over the noise of the train.

"I've been looking for you."

The sack was roughly jerked down again but not before he heard the sound of a loading door being slid open on this freight car.

His world was suddenly filled with rushing wind and the ear-splitting rattling noises of a rapidly moving freight train and the occasional dinging of warning bells as they rushed through rural crossings.

His chair tipped back on its rear legs.

He was being dragged, the legs of the chair scraping across the metal floor of the freight car.

He tried to kick his feet but the restraints did their job well so he violently thrashed from side to side in the chair trying to break free.

The chair stopped.

The wind and the sounds were more intense and more frightening. *I must be at the door,* he thought, in full panic.

"Now!" came a shout, and he and his chair briefly floated through the noisy air, smashing back first into a concrete bridge abutment that carried the tracks over a wide stream.

The impact of the abutment shattered the back slats of the chair. The arms of the chair separated from the rest of it and then the whole mess splashed awkwardly into the muddy foulness of the creek.

The cacophony of the train continued on, and then a sudden silence in the creek.

His arms were still tied to what remained of the chair but he could move them and his legs somehow had come free. He ripped the sack off his head and the tape off his mouth, sucking air and blinking his eyes. He was able to swim and use the chair's arms as makeshift oars as he thrashed in the darkness desperately hoping to touch land before he drowned.

His tethered hands finally scraped mud and he stood up. It was so dark that he might as well have still been hooded. He looked back and forth trying to understand where he was.

The stench of the creek made him long for the odor of the burlap. *I'm in sewage,* he thought, spitting out whatever drops he'd just sucked in, still standing knee deep in the miserable creek.

His eyes slowly adjusted to the dark. He began to focus and could see the outline of the railroad bridge silhouetted against a soft glow of city lights in the distance and blinking red lights on three towers lined up on the horizon blinking in sequence: left, middle, right.

He discerned that the towers belonged to the local radio station. Jenkins knew where he was.

He scrambled on all fours through the mud and the rocks and climbed the embankment up to the tracks. He sat on a rail for a moment in the silent darkness, his head still hurting and his back aching from slamming into the bridge but otherwise not injured. He worried about how much of the stinking water he ingested and wondered when he would start puking.

He sat in his soaked clothing and felt something crawl up his leg.

He quickly stood to pull down his pants and flicked away whatever the creature was.

He looked both ways. He could tell from which direction the train and his captors had brought him.

He began walking in that direction.

As his mind cleared it became clear to him that only one person could arrange for him to be tossed from that train.

And that person would not accept failure.

With every step down the darkened tracks, it became clearer that he had to get to that person, quickly.

CHAPTER SEVENTEEN

The old man sat in his chair on the porch.

There weren't many days left when he could enjoy evenings on his porch as the season began to turn to autumn and the trees at the highest elevations started to transition to their fall splendor. He truly loved this place.

He would remain at this house until the skies were gray and the chilled winds blew from the north and the forecast began to hint at snow. He would then return to the city and spend the days at his desk counting how many cigarettes he sold each day to his hacking and coughing customers worldwide.

Until then, he would enjoy every minute of these late-summer evenings when the temperature dropped more quickly, the small creatures who lived in his yard would be seen less frequently and the twinkling lights on the nearby mountains would flicker on earlier and earlier.

He sent the staff home for the day and quietly told one of them that he wouldn't need her on this night. She was disappointed; she enjoyed the attention and needed the money. There would be other nights.

He was enjoying his drink and a cigar on the porch of the quiet house as the soft evening light across the valley began to fade when he heard footsteps on his porch.

Smitty approached, pointed to a chair, and the old man nodded.

Smitty sat, and took a deep breath.

"Everything go ok?" the old man asked.

"Yes, boss, everything is handled," Smitty said, staring at the folded hands in his lap.

"Jenkins?"

"Gone."

"The train engineers?"

"Also gone."

"The missing boxcars?"

"On a dead spur in the hills."

"Whatdya mean a dead spur?"

"One of the guys hid them on an abandoned track up in the foothills," Smitty explained calmly.

The old man smiled.

"Just leave 'em there; not worth the trouble and the attention," he said. "How'd you find them, anyway?'

Smitty smiled almost bashfully and then talked for a half hour about how he followed Robbie across the state and figured out where everybody was. He described the different ways he took care of all the old man's problems. He glossed over the details like the ambush at the short-line shop but left out no other details of the story he told with great enthusiasm about Jenkins's demise and the irony of tossing him from a train.

The old man barely listened.

He knew more than Smitty, a lot more.

He didn't care about the cigarettes or the railcars. And he didn't care about the people except to know that Smitty had handled them and they would never bother him again. He smiled to himself at Jenkins's sophisticated planning, the audacity of the plan and wondered how much Jenkins had actually gotten away with.

But he didn't really care about any of it. It was actually a sad, depressing mess. He was hurt by the betrayal of one of his loyal people, but he could move on.

"Boss?" Smitty asked softly.

"What?" the old man replied.

"How'd you know?"

The old man sighed and took a sip of his drink.

"How'd I know what?" he asked.

"How'd you know it was them guys?"

"You mean Jenkins and the others?" said the old man.

"Yessir, that part never made sense to me," Smitty said.

The old man thought for a minute about whether to tell him anything at all.

Before he could reply, Smitty continued.

"How'd you figure it out?"

The old man turned and looked at Smitty and reflected on all the events of recent weeks.

"It started with a visit," the old man said, head slumped on his chest. "From someone who made all this possible."

He looked up and waved a shaky hand across his valley and his mountains.

The visitor was an old acquaintance in New York, he told Smitty.

It was a relationship from decades ago when the old man was still young, trying to start his enterprise and the soldiers coming home wanted more cigarettes than he could make. He was losing the battle and needed capital to buy more machines to make his cigarettes.

The young man begged all the big banks in New York but they rejected him.

The long-ago friend was the only banker who said yes.

They met by chance in a bar near Times Square while the young man was fishing for money in the big city.

The young man was smoking one of his cigarettes and the sweet aroma caught the attention of the banker who was part of a large family in New York who owned a bank that was laundering money for organized crime. Over several gin martinis he and the young man agreed that pouring cash into cigarette-rolling machines was a clever way to wash some cash. They joined forces, greatly enriching them both.

As Smitty listened the old man continued.

The banker from his past recently appeared on the front steps of the old man's mansion, uninvited.

It was not a social visit.

The banker sat in the old man's parlor and reminded him about how he financed his business originally and how uncomfortable it would be for the world which admired him to learn he'd originally capitalized his fledgling business with mob money.

"All I need is some product for my colleagues to sell," the banker said to him. "They need a substantial shipment and they aren't interested in your wholesale price."

"What are they interested in?" the old man asked the banker, knowing the answer.

"Why don't you send somebody to work it out with my colleagues?" the banker replied. "You and I don't need to get our hands dirty."

The old man reflected on that conversation and now looked at Smitty who was staring at him with wide eyes.

"So," the old man said sadly, "I had to figure out something."

He paused for a moment, unsure of whether to continue.

He told Smitty that the heist had been planned on this back porch, in the very chairs where the two of them sat tonight.

"I knew Jenkins was up to something," he said. "He acted strangely at times about some of the business so I was concerned that he wasn't honest with me. I knew just enough that I had him cornered and I knew he wouldn't say no to me."

He continued telling his story.

He said Jenkins confessed that he knew of some small-time thefts from their trains that didn't amount to anything. It was actually Jenkins's idea to nab those thieves and force them to help organize a larger theft that could be sold to the Jersey mob. Insurance would cover the losses and the mob would pay discretely for the stolen smokes. The old man's coffers would get a double dip of cash and everybody would be happy, especially his banker friend.

He paused to catch his breath.

"It was me," he finally said, sadly. "I did it. I hope you don't begrudge me."

Smitty said nothing, unsure of what to make of what he just heard.

"It would look like a big-time train robbery," the old man said, "but we had lots of help with the logistics that Jenkins and his trainmen never knew about. That's why it worked so smoothly. And then, everybody who was a part of it would disappear. That part was sad but necessary.

"The only part that didn't work smoothly was the money," the old man continued. "That's when I knew Jenkins was rotten."

And, now, the old man thought, what to do about the only one left who knew anything, perhaps too much, including literally where the bodies were buried, and now knew everything.

Smitty could see that his boss was deeply troubled.

He leaned over and put his hand on his boss's knee. He looked at him with compassion, unsure of what to say next that would comfort him.

The old man flinched slightly at Smitty's touch, and shifted in his chair.

The sound of the single shot to Smitty's chest echoed loudly but was lost in the vastness of the old man's world. He calmly set his pistol on the table next to his drink unbothered that anyone heard it.

The old man lifted his drink and tipped it in

the direction of Smitty's bloody and still twitching body, a toast for a job well done, a life well-lived, a life that now had ended.

He took a sip. While the glass was still at his lips he saw movement, something at the end of the porch.

He reached for his pistol.

"Don't even," said Jenkins, stepping from the shadows.

The old man froze, and gasped.

"What...what, I mean, huh? I thought you were ..."

"Dead? Or missing? Or drowned in some filthy creek? Guess what, I'm none of those things!"

The old man clutched the arms of his chair unsure of what to do as Jenkins moved toward him. Jenkins had a gun and it was pointed at the old man who knew he would die instantly if he made a move for his own gun.

"I heard every word you just said to Smitty," Jenkins said.

The old man gasped and rocked back in his chair as the blood drained from his face.

"Come with me," Jenkins growled.

"No, please," the old man begged, panic

growing inside. "Whatever you want, we can work it out."

Jenkins ignored him.

"I'll make you a rich man!" the old man. "Please! I'm begging you!"

Jenkins snorted. "I'm already a rich man, asshole."

Jenkins clutched the arms of the old man. He resisted violently, and flung his body back and forth as he tried to fight out of Jenkins's grasp.

The struggle was brief. He was quickly out of breath and no match for Jenkins who strong-armed him down the porch's side steps, around to the rear of the house and to the expansive parking area where on happier nights luxury cars parked after bringing the area's rich and powerful to dine at the old man's table and drink his elegant wines.

This evening, only a single car was there.

"Get in," Jenkins ordered again, opening the front passenger door to the old man's Lincoln.

The old man resisted again and struggled briefly to free himself, then resigned to do as he was told.

Jenkins leaned in and knocked him unconscious with the butt of his pistol.

The old man collapsed in the floor of the

Lincoln's huge front seat. Jenkins had to shift the unconscious body when he slid into the drivers' seat.

Jenkins turned the car toward the main road and looked over his shoulder certain that neither of them would ever see this place again.

EPILOGUE

FIVE YEARS LATER

On rare days when he felt nostalgic or bored, Jenkins pulled the newspaper clippings from the box in the front closet.

The scandal surrounding the old man's tragic death filled the newspapers for months and kept them filled for years after that with stories of the impact on those to whom his wealth was bequeathed.

The initial stories announced in dramatic headlines the shocking death of the cigarette baron in an auto accident, his big Lincoln wrapped around a tree in a hairpin turn on the twisting road that wound crazily from his mountain house down to the village below.

The local firefighters were indiscreet gossips who quickly told everyone that the old man had been drinking and eagerly described in gory detail how his body was so mangled in the wreck that nobody could've survived. The fire department displayed the dramatic wreckage of the Lincoln behind the fire station for months as a warning to young people about drinking and driving. They left the dried blood on the floorboard to reinforce the point.

The shock of the wreck was quickly eclipsed by the news that the old man's personal servant had been found shot to death on the back porch of the big house and was still sitting in his chair, eyes wide open in shock, when the staff arrived for work the next morning.

Was this a lover's spat gone horribly bad? A business deal gone wrong? Tongues wagged for weeks and spun up deliciously obscene but unfounded tales of what was going on between those two.

The funeral was worthy of a head of state with an overflow crowd at the university's massive chapel. Some came to mourn but most were there to gawk at the rich and famous who attended. The newspapers and radio stations covered it and the local tv station had its most famous name broadcasting live which was a rarity at the time. It was the biggest news of the day and every story repeated the salacious details of the old man's untimely demise and the gruesome death of his manservant.

A newspaper reporter surreptitiously followed the grief-stricken family to the cemetery for the private burial hoping to observe something that would add context to his funeral coverage. The next morning, his newspaper's front page had the reporter's sensational story of the scene at the gravesite when the old man's evil and estranged daughters discovered that the family's cemetery plot had an unknown occupant planted next to their dear departed mother. The reporter's story described in great detail the shrieking and arm-waving of the daughters when the gravestone of the interloper revealed her to be a very young woman who was buried with an unnamed infant. According to the story, one of the daughters fainted in the cemetery when she realized that the grave filled with the mysterious young woman's remains was the plot her father had reserved for her.

Jenkins smiled when he read for the

umpteenth time the yellowing newspaper report about the details of the old man's will that were leaked to the enterprising reporter who had covered the high drama at the grave site. The will was over a hundred pages with specific bequests for life-changing endowments for universities and hospitals, generous payments for his house staff and stable boys and plenty of funds for Daisy and Strawberry to live their best lives. A peculiar bequest was a lifetime annuity for one of the housekeepers and a scholarship program for her son.

Also leaked to the reporter was a detailed eyewitness description of the reaction of the hateful and deranged daughters who suffered another indignity when their names went unmentioned during the reading of their father's will. It was reported the daughters began fighting with each other in the lawyer's office each blaming the other for doing cruel things to their father that resulted in the denial of their birthright. The daughter whose assigned place for perpetual rest was occupied by a stranger conceded the fight when her blonde wig was ripped off by her sister to reveal a rat's nest of straw-colored hair that resembled a mop used to clean up vomit.

Jenkins couldn't get enough so he thumbed through other fading news clippings that he'd read many times.

The old man's board of directors stumbled around for a long time before they could figure out how to replace him as the company's stock spiraled into oblivion. Jenkins was naturally one of the finalists but they couldn't find him to interview him so they moved on. His grieving and fearful family never heard from him again so they presumed him to be dead and eventually moved on with their lives which were comfortably financed by the cigarette company.

There was a clipping from The Wall Street Journal that the accounting firm hired by the board to figure out the cigarette factory's finances found thousands of irregularities including millions of dollars in payments to make-believe companies. The FBI was brought in and a half dozen young lawyers around the country were tracked down and indicted on fraud charges. Jenkins was indicted but it was irrelevant because he was nowhere to be found and the cigarette company responded by canceling the monthly checks to his sad and now impoverished little family.

After reminiscing long enough, Jenkins would return the fading clippings to their place in the front closet and step out onto his front porch overlooking the magnificent blue waters of the Grenadines in the southern Caribbean.

His home was on one of the few elevated hills in the entire Caribbean and he could see nearly one hundred eighty degrees of beauty as he moved about the wrap-around porch. There was always a stiff, warm refreshing breeze and enormous iguanas eating bugs in the yard.

Every morning was remarkable and on this one a graceful four-masted schooner sailed by in the distance through the brilliant ocean punctuated by small, bright whitecaps.

Strangely, he mused, he never thought about the little family he abandoned nor the mansion by the tracks nor the long, tedious train rides to the old man's house on the mountain. He never thought about his children and whether they were good kids or if they might be in college by now or if they were dead or alive.

He regretted nothing.

He had coldly flipped a switch. That part of this life had been turned off.

He had a new life now.

Nobody could find his money and nobody could find him.

If anyone tried to find him, a phalanx of highly compensated people on the mainland and at the island's docks would sound the alert and were qualified to make whomever was poking around simply disappear.

By mid-morning on most days, his live-in girlfriend emerged lazily from the house. She moved elegantly to her poolside lounge chair covered with a luxurious towel. On the small table next to it was her first bloody mary of the day (light on the clamato), whatever tabloid magazine she was reading at the moment and a small coke bottle.

She stretched gracefully in the sun, like a cat. She usually felt the desire to be naked on the pool deck, just because she could.

He was delighted to have her company and always kissed her warmly as she settled in for the morning.

She returned his kisses just as warmly.

But before any kisses, she always graciously removed from her lips an ever-present unfiltered Camel which she dropped into the coke bottle where its faint sizzle reminded her of how far she'd come.

This was their life.

It never changed.

THE END

CHAOS ON THE CANAL

A SHORT STORY

GENE UPCHURCH

Based on actual events ... sort of

PART I

Jean-Claude quickly finished a lunch croissant at his desk at the Paris law firm that his father founded, handed his secretary a stack of papers to sort out and bid her farewell.

He cranked the Audi A8 and smoothly navigated the madness of Parisian traffic on his way to a four-day holiday.

He pointed the big Audi toward Dijon where he would meet Madeline in a couple of hours.

This would be their first holiday together, and first night as a couple. She was barely twenty-five, nearly half his age, and his heartbeat quickened at the thought of a young, classic French beauty lying next to him.

Madeline had grown up in a wealthy family with a father who was passionate about boating with a special love for barging on the Canal du Central in the Burgundy region of central France.

Her father had sold his barge years earlier and died the previous summer. Over a martini on their first date, Madeline told Jean-Claude the summers on her father's barge were the happiest of her life.

With Madeline now elegantly gracing the passenger seat of the Audi, they spent a couple of hours in light and sometimes flirty conversation as they drove south into wine country.

Madeline was entertaining Jean-Claude with a funny story about shopping for clothes in Paris and unaware they had just crossed an arched green bridge into the beautiful village of St. Leger-sur-Dheune when she looked out the windshield and sat up in her seat.

"The canal!" she shouted, hands to her face. "My beloved canal! I miss her so much!"

Jean-Claude turned on to the street fronting the historic canal, and then into a parking lot.

"Jean-Claude!" she exclaimed, "have you done this for me?"

Lined up in front of them were seven gleaming weekender barges.

Jean-Claude put his hand on her shoulder.

"The one on the far left," he said, "is ours for the next four days."

She hugged him warmly, then sprang from the car and pranced to the dock where their barge awaited them.

Their gear was loaded, champagne was poured and he expertly guided the barge into the canal for he too came from a family of boaters so the operation of the barge was no obstacle for him.

Jean-Claude planned to sail past a couple of villages and moor at a quiet spot along the canal. But the combination of delicious champagne and mutual desire forced an early mooring so he quickly tied up the boat and joined an eager Madeline in the barge's master suite for the night.

He slept blissfully and dreamed of Madeline.

Suddenly, a scream jarred him awake.

He sat upright. He looked around.

The other side of the bed was empty.

He was disoriented and frightened. He lived alone so he was unaccustomed to the noise of another person much less awakening to screams.

Soft sunlight drifted past curtains they had

neglected to close amid the passionate distractions of the night.

Another horrifying scream.

He leapt from the tousled bed and rushed to the bow of the barge.

Madeline was there, hands to her face. She looked at him in terror, and pointed.

He blinked in confusion, unable to process what he saw.

On the bank of the canal was an obviously dead body, the upper half of which was nearly obscured by the lush green grass and the lower half obscured by the murky brown water of the canal. The body appeared to be that of a corpulent elderly man, a blue walking stick clutched in his right hand. A crow picked at his unseeing left eye.

A few feet away, floating face down in the canal, was the body of a woman, her hair the color of a cheap broom.

The gendarmes were summoned and quickly arrived in their little station wagons, revolving blue lights flashing in alarm.

Jean-Claude and Madeline clutched one another and shivered in the morning chill as the first gendarmes to arrive cautiously approached the grisly scene. They were accustomed to dealing with pickpockets and petty thieves but not discovery of dead bodies in their usually tranquil canal. Jean-Claude silently observed that they were hesitant to approach the scene and were clearly overwhelmed by the circumstances. One of them threw up in some bushes.

It took a few minutes, but the gendarmes gathered themselves and secured the scene with yellow tape. They then moved away from the bodies as far as they could and still be professional. They stood watch until their sergeant arrived.

He was less reluctant to approach the putrid mess in the canal. He stepped with great purpose to the rotting corpses where he squatted down to gaze closely at what was left of them.

After a brief investigation, the gendarme sergeant approached the shaken Jean-Claude and Madeline.

"Our investigation is not complete," he said solemnly. "It's unclear if this was an accident or a crime. We have many questions."

He continued.

"These victims may be British tourists whose family has not heard from them. They were booked on a luxury barge, so we will have to track down that barge and have a go at the folks on it to see what they may know."

The sergeant stopped for a moment, lost in his thoughts.

"You know," he said, scratching his chin, "British tourists stay drunk most of the time when they're on holiday so they may have fallen overboard. And, since everyone despises British tourists, someone may have given them a toss."

He turned and looked over his shoulder at the scene where the bloated corpses were being dragged out of the canal and into the coroner's waiting van.

"Enjoy the rest of your holiday," the sergeant said, his gaze resting upon the magnificent cleavage of the young Madeline. "I'll ring you if I need you."

PART II

The laughter from the barge could be heard through the open windows of the tidy beige villas in the little town of Remigny that clung to the side of the *Canal de Central.*

The local folks were accustomed to the sounds from the canal and, over the years, their lives had become synced with the comings and goings of the slow-moving barges that crept past their homes and occasionally moored near the green bridge that connected their little world to everywhere else.

In a different era, the barges hauled goats and coal from one end of the region to the other, the goats to be slaughtered and the coal to be burned, all part of the thriving commerce of central France at that time. The canals were built during Napoleon's reign to facilitate the efficient movement of troops who crowded onto barges that were towed by mules on well-worn paths alongside the canal. These paths were now paved so that arrogant French bicyclists could hurtle through the countryside on their fancy bikes and harass the ignorant tourists who didn't know what was going on.

The barges were now elegant floating hotels that hauled wealthy tourists who spent thousands of Euros per week to gawk at the farmers and villagers along the canal and tour the wineries and other attractions along the fifty-mile route. The locals laughed at the dumb tourists who spent so much money and time going two kilometers per hour through the canal when they could see everything they wished in an automobile in a half a day.

On this breathtakingly beautiful evening, the barge named *Princesse de la Gourmandise* was moored along a grassy strip that separated Remigny from the canal.

The passengers were on their second round of cocktails and enjoying the experience. Nobody had to drive anywhere, and the farthest anyone had to travel tonight was down a short flight of stairs to the luxurious suites awaiting them belowdecks.

One of the suites was empty, so if one of the couples had a drunk fight or needed to escape from a noisy snorer the crew had left the door unlocked and the young captain, with a laugh, cautioned against illicit rendezvouses.

The passengers looked at one another as if such a thing was remotely possible, then simultaneously burst out laughing at the outrageousness of the idea.

Their laughter was contagious, and the local villagers wondered what was so funny.

There were six of them, all from the States, and five crew members from around the world all under the age of twenty-five, except for the classically trained French chef who now was putting the final touches on a sauce he had specially created for the roast duck that was finishing in the oven.

Three bottles of Burgundian wine were

already breathing on the outdoor patio where the happy passengers would dine tonight, a classic white and a couple of reds. It was likely that others would be uncorked as the evening progressed.

They drank their cocktails, snacked on hors d 'oeuvres that included a freshly-made pate the chef bought this afternoon at a market in Remigny after the barge arrived.

This was the best evening of the trip.

"May I come aboard?"

The laughter stopped as the entire population of the barge whipped their heads toward the gangplank.

A gendarme sergeant stood in the grass at the end of the gangplank. He held out his badge.

"Captain, I have most urgent business. May I come aboard?" he asked.

The young captain was French and had shared with some of the passengers his background and experience. To be so young, he had accomplished much in the complicated world of ships and sailing and possessed the poise and demeanor of a real leader. It was actually surprising that someone with his qualifications was taking a turn commanding a barge that barely moved but it was clear that he was delighted with where he was in his life. And, it was obvious to all that the attractive blonde hostess who was barely twenty spent more nights in his cabin than in the one she was assigned to share with the barge's other hostess.

"What is your business?" the young captain asked the sergeant.

"I have questions for your crew and passengers regarding missing persons," the sergeant replied.

The laughter stopped.

The mood on the deck suddenly was solemn.

The passengers looked at one another. No one changed their expression. Then they looked at their young captain, waiting for him to reply to the sergeant.

The captain looked at his passengers with resignation, shrugged his shoulders and motioned the sergeant aboard.

"My apologies for interrupting or delaying your dinner," he said, looking at the elegantly prepared table that awaited its diners.

The chef emerged from the cabin, hands on hips, rage in his eyes. The roast duck had to be served promptly and at the perfect temperature.

Timing was everything! Any delay was an outrageous affront to his effort!

The sergeant looked at the small gathering, still standing with cocktails in hand, and told them what had been found on the banks of the canal.

PART III

The passengers had gathered a few days earlier in the lobby of a prestigious hotel in the historic downtown area of Dijon. This was the gathering point where a van and driver would collect them for the short trip to the canal, the first step of their long-awaited barge cruise.

As each couple entered the lobby, they were excitedly asked, "Are you on *the Princesse de la Gourmandise*?"

If the answer was yes, introductions were made and inquiries made about where everyone lived.

Judgments were made immediately. Only four

couples would be on the barge, so it would be intimate.

The British couple was the last to arrive. The male partner of the pair limped into the lobby with a blue cane in one hand and a small satchel in the other. His wife trailed him straining to pull two enormous rolling suitcases.

"I must have the front seat," the British man demanded loudly in a thick brogue before saying good morning or introducing himself to anyone. "As you can see, I have an affliction and simply cannot get in and out of the rear of the vehicle."

The other passengers looked at one another, shoulders slumped with disappointment. *So, he's gonna be one of those,* they all thought.

After a few awkward moments, he finally introduced himself to his fellow passengers as Brian and allowed his wife, Hilary, to introduce herself.

They immediately began tell of their previous travels on other barges, river boats and cruise ships and how worried they were that *the Princesse de la Gourmandise* would not measure up.

After what seemed an interminable wait, the driver from the barge arrived and everyone excitedly made their way to the van, where the driver hoisted Brian's crippled body into the coveted front seat.

The thirty-minute drive seemed like two hours as Brian and Hilary talked non-stop about all their travels and were especially obsessed with a trip aboard a barge named *Renaissance,* which Hilary pronounced *Ray-NAY-Saunce* in her irritating thick accent. It was *Ray-NAY-Saunce* this and *Ray-NAY-Saunce* that with Brian frequently interrupting to add commentary or to correct Hilary until van mercifully arrived at the canal where their floating hotel for the next six nights awaited them.

The passengers met the crew and briefly freshened up, eager to get back to the upper deck where a marvelous party had been prepared to celebrate their arrival. There was a safety briefing by the captain and the bar was opened.

And then it continued.

More jabbering from the Brits about their beloved *Ray-NAY-Saunce* now that they'd had five minutes to compare it to the *Princesse de la Gourmandise.* Their current vessel was smaller than the marvelous *Ray-NAY-Saunce* and they wondered how such a small kitchen could meet their sophisticated needs that had been so marveously satisfied aboard the magnificent *Ray-NAY-Saunce*.

"I must sit at the head of the table," Brian announced when they were called to dinner which was to be served outside at a table that had been beautifully prepared. "I need extra room because of my affliction, and this must be the case at every meal."

Hilary added, "The people on the *Ray-NAY-Saunce* were so supportive of Brian. "They were happy for him to sit at the head of the table."

The other passengers gave each other the side eye and shook their heads at the prospects of six days of this crap.

It got worse.

Visits to every winery and museum slowed to a glacial pace and were altered to accommodate Brian's swollen and twisted legs including arrangements for a staff person to follow him around with a folding chair so he could sit when the host would pause the tour briefly to explain something important.

At one of Burgundy's most prestigious wineries, the lovely and intelligent and interesting hostess could barely get a word in because Brian thought the group would want to hear about how this winery compared to one that he and his witch-faced wife had visited in New Zealand.

"I want to hear what *she* has to say, not you!" one his fellow passengers finally snapped at Brian who appeared to not understand what the fuss was about.

Nevertheless, the van ride back to the barge was made in icy silence.

The last straw came at dinner that night.

Hilary announced that everyone's departure time on the final morning would be four hours earlier than planned because she and Brian wished to catch an earlier train to return to the luxurious comfort of their flat in London. This meant everyone else would unnecessarily arise pre-dawn to accommodate the Brits and then wait around for hours and hours for their own transport.

"Oh hell no!" shouted Leeza, one of the passengers from North Carolina, a serrated steak knife gripped tightly in her right hand and, in her left, a vodka martini the remnants of which she threw into the shocked face of Hilary.

Leeza continued to make her point.

"We will NOT be inconvenienced by you inconsiderate ass wipes just so you can get home a little earlier than planned!" she yelled. "We have been patient while you have commandeered this whole trip and we're sick of it. What is WRONG with you?"

Silence fell upon the barge.

Something had to be done.

Trey and Gregg, friends from North Carolina and on the *Princesse de la Gourmandise* with their wives, one of whom had just flung the dregs of a martini into the face of Hilary, moved to a far corner of the deck, fresh drinks in hand, and agreed on a plan to be implemented the next evening.

They told no one.

It was elegant in its simplicity.

Trey suffered occasionally from kidney stones, the pain of which can be compared to a woman's protracted labor of overweight triplets gripping sewing needles in their tiny newborn hands as they emerged from unspeakable parts of their mother's anatomy. He always traveled with an assortment of medicines to help him deal with the excruciating pain of an attack should one occur. The most powerful tool in his pain-killing arsenal was a thirty pack of five hundred milligram codeine tablets.

The plan, such as it was, was to slip the Brits enough codeine so they'd stay in their cabin for a couple of days, shut the fuck up and leave everyone alone. Neither Trey nor Gregg had any idea how many tablets it would take so they swore to one another that they would carefully monitor the dispensing of the medicine.

The next evening was lovely under a full French moon as Trey and Gregg assumed the roles of gracious hosts, bartenders and pharmacists. They served drinks and wine to the Brits who swilled their poisoned concoctions with zeal.

Unsurprisingly, Trey and Gregg also fell drunk and naturally lost track of who had served Brian and Hilary and how much they'd been served.

Trey and Gregg stepped aside to confer.

Trey inspected the box of codeine.

It was empty.

They looked at each other, somewhat concerned.

Thirty tablets in the flabby British bellies.

"Oops," Trey said, eyebrows raised.

"Oh dear," Gregg said, his words slightly slurred so it sounded like he said "Odor."

At that moment, Brian raised his hand at his usual seat at the head of the table as if to be recognized for a speech.

"Mah olip guj xirt sigl," he shouted defiantly and slammed his hand on the table, overturning a half-filled wine glass, sloshing its contents onto the fine clothes of some of his annoyed table mates.

He tried to spew out some additional gibberish but his eyes suddenly went blank and his mouth stopped working except to expel a thimbleful of vomit.

As the other passengers held their collective breath at what calamity might occur next, Brian plummeted with great drama face down into the puff pastry that had taken all afternoon to be baked by the chef who would be monstrously displeased that his magnificent creation was now the resting place of Brian's corpulent snout.

The other passengers froze at the sight of this spectacle.

Hilary reached out to comfort her dear husband who was obviously having a spot of trouble. But her brain was so short-circuited that she lovingly caressed not her distressed husband but the table's elegant, floral centerpiece before collapsing back into her chair and nearly sliding into the floor, a long thread of filthy spittle dangling from her mouth.

She muttered something incomprehensible about the *Re-nay-saunce*, but she only got as far as *Re-nay* before her eyes rolled back in her head and she spoke no more.

"What a mess," Trey said quietly to Gregg and they both shrugged their shoulders as if to say, "*Oh well.*"

The rest of the group looked knowingly at one another and slinked off to the relative sanity of their cabins leaving the British couple alone in their tortured slumber.

Trey and Gregg also went below and waited a few minutes before returning to the upper deck.

The codeine couple hadn't moved and the crew apparently had gone into hiding without clearing the table which was understandable considering the unconscious obstacles blocking their way.

Trey and Gregg looked at each other.

Their plan had worked, or at least it seemed so. It was clearly going to be a while, if ever, before Brian and Hilary uttered any more tiresome drivel.

But they hadn't really thought through the consequences of, let's say, killing them.

Brian hadn't moved since face planting into the chef's beloved pastry. Trey put two fingers to Brian's clammy, damp neck but he didn't really know what he was doing. He didn't feel a pulse, but wasn't entirely sure.

"I've never been around that many dead people except for the old farts who eat lunch together every Friday at our club, but these two look pretty dead to me," Gregg said, glaring at Trey. "I didn't sign on for this shit. "

"You can count as good as me," Trey replied impatiently. "Whose idea was it to hand out dangerous narcotics like Halloween candy? That whole box of pills would kill a fat hog."

They paused for a moment to laugh at that comparison.

"I wonder if the bar is still open," Gregg said, looking longingly at the liquor cabinet in the cabin."

"C'mon man, we gotta clean this mess up, if you know what I mean," Trey said.

"I never know what you're talking about," Gregg said. "And another thing. If you write one of your bullshit, nonsense stories about this please don't use my real name. In fact, leave me out of it altogether."

Trey ignored Gregg's demand as he spotted Gregg's iPad on the table, sparking an idea.

"I need you to google how to dispose of overdose victims," Trey said.

"I would be happy to," Gregg said, not thinking clearly that such a search could land him in prison. "But I don't have a connection. Haven't since we left home. I save a lot of money with my wireless plan but it doesn't work beyond my front yard."

"But you've been staring at it for nearly a week," Trey said. "What've you been looking at?"

"Solitaire!"

"Good lord," Trey said. "Grab a fat arm and let's get these pigs outta here."

It took them a half hour to drag the Brits through the darkness of the warm French night about a hundred yards down the tow path behind where the *Princesse de la Gourmandise* was moored. Brian was the most difficult because he weighed as much as an elephant seal and was about as flabby.

They dragged his lumpy carcass as far as they could but couldn't get him all the way in the canal. Hilary was easier to dump in the canal.

At dawn, the captain of the *Princesse de la Gourmandise* started her small diesel engine and slowly moved from her mooring on to her next stop.

PART IV

The sergeant continued his questions.

"So, no one noticed they were missing. Is that what you're saying?"

He looked at the passengers, and then to the crew.

Everyone nodded in agreement.

He turned to the captain.

"And you acknowledge, sir, that you were moored less than a half mile from where we found their bodies?"

The captain nodded in agreement.

"That's correct. We always moor at that spot. The company has an arrangement with the village that compensates it for allowing us to spend the night," the captain said.

"Do you have surveillance cameras?" the sergeant asked.

"Why, of course," replied the captain.

Trey and Gregg quietly stopped breathing and tried not to faint.

"Excellent," said the sergeant.

"But they don't work," the captain said. "Something about the blue tooth link. We've never been able to get them to work. We don't even know what blue tooth is."

The sergeant's shoulders slumped.

Suddenly the French chef burst through the door of the cabin and onto the deck, a huge knife in his hand.

'MY FUCKING DUCK MUST BE SERVED NOW!" he shouted, glaring at the sergeant.

"I'm afraid you are inconveniencing my passengers and must go," the captain said quietly. "We have no information that will help you. We don't know what happened."

Leeza said, "I've got a great duck joke that I'll tell when everybody calms the fuck down. But I'll need two more glasses of wine if I'm gonna tell it right."

The sergeant, however, was not finished.

"A final question, then I'll leave you," he said. "Were they drinking heavily when you last saw them?"

"Everybody on this barge is a heavy drinker," the captain replied with a wry smile. "I've never seen anything like it. These people are professional drinkers, especially the two couples from North Carolina. We've had to resupply liquor and wine twice already. But that's beside the point. When I last saw the victims, they had passed out on the deck. From there, who knows?"

The sergeant nodded respectfully to the young captain and, in doing so, clearly acknowledged that nothing further could be accomplished by continuing to pester these nice people.

"I will leave you now and disturb you no further," he said to the group as the chef glared at him. "But before I take my leave, may I please be allowed to use your guest toilette?"

"We don't have one," the captain said in the classic impatient French manner, with lots of shoulder shrugging and hand waving. "If the guests are willing, they may allow you to use the loo in one of their cabins.

The guests looked at one another and shrugged their own shoulders. *What's the harm?*

The captain motioned to the stairs leading down to guest cabins.

The sergeant bowed from the waist in gratitude and went downstairs entering the first cabin he came to. He went into the elegant and well-appointed toilette which was larger than the one in his apartment. He looked longingly at the comfortable toilet seat and thought about how wonderful it would be to spend an hour there with a good book.

But obviously there was no time for such tempting pleasures of the bowels. He needed to take care of his business and leave these people alone

As he zipped his trousers from a satisfying piss, his eye fell to an object in the small brass trash can next to the toilet.

He bent down for a closer look.

"These people are mine now," he growled to himself followed by a maniacal chuckle as he slipped the object into his jacket pocket, returned to the main cabin and bid a good night to the restless group on deck.

PART V

The lieutenant of the gendarmerie station looked at his sergeant with the weary dejection of someone who has not seen everything but has seen too much.

"No," he said emphatically, a deep sigh punctuating his message. "You've spent too much time on a couple of stoned, dead Brits who mixed so much whisky, wine and pills that they killed their stupid selves. There's no crime here. Get back to work on some actual crimes."

On the desk between them was the empty box of codeine pills removed from the brass trash can on the barge by the sergeant after his post-piss discovery.

"But lieutenant, this box wasn't in the Brits' cabin and the prescription is for one of the other passengers!" exclaimed the sergeant. "I think they were murdered and this empty box of pills will prove it!"

The lieutenant rolled his eyes. He lacked the resources to chase down real criminals. And now his sergeant wanted to take time away from real work to meddle in the deaths of a couple of Brits who probably did themselves in with drugs and drink.

It would be one thing if the deceased were French.

But Brits? Who cares?

"No," he said again and, with a majestic motion, swiped the empty codeine box into his desk-side waste basket.

"Now, move on."

PART VI

Trey was on Gregg's doorstep, his iPad in hand.

Unlike Gregg, Trey's technology was world class and worked everywhere, even when he was out of sight of his home.

"Have you seen this?" Trey asked, shoving the iPad at Gregg.

Gregg took the device and quickly scanned a story reported by a London tabloid that apparently had been swirling through social media. Gregg might've been up to date on world affairs if his home computer was connected to the internet. He kept banging on the "enter" key but nothing ever happened.

Anyway, it was the story about the mysterious circumstances of the deaths of a British couple who disappeared while on a luxury barge cruise through the Burgundy region of France.

The whole sordid mess had become an international scandal as the British government accused the French of ignoring the obvious murders of two of the kingdom's citizens and refused to thoroughly investigate this horrible crime.

The tabloid gleefully reported how several Members of Parliament demanded that the Prime Minister dispatch without delay and with the upmost urgency one of the Royal Navy's most powerful and well-armed warships, preferably one with nuclear weapons if the Kingdom had such things, to the canal where this disgraceful incident occurred as a show of strength to the weak, pathetic and indifferent French people.

The Admiralty sent a firm but dignified missive to the delusional and moronic MPs that such an action would probably ignite another wasteful war between the two long-time adversaries. And, he added, the Royal Navy lacks any vessel small enough to fit into the canal except for perhaps a warship's lifeboat which would unlikely send the type of threatening message to the recalcitrant French government that the ignorant MPs thought would be useful.

The only person in France who cared about finding the truth was the gendarme sergeant. After months of dead ends and lack of support from his entire nation, he provided information to the British in hopes that her leaders would have an interest in finding the killers of Brian and Hilary, if indeed there had been some killers.

The tabloid reported with great enthusiasm that this effort by the sergeant backfired spectacularly as his fellow countrymen and women viewed him as a filthy traitor and could care less about the meaningless demise of two unknown Brits.

The tabloid kept stoking the fire because it sold newspapers and was excellent internet clickbait. The whole mess became inflamed beyond reason.

It was too much for the sergeant, and he slipped down a rat hole of insanity.

"I know who did it," the sergeant was quoted by the tabloid as saying, accompanied by a full-page photo of him being escorted from the station house by two of his colleagues, one on each arm, his feet dragging on the cobblestones, a crazed look in his eyes as he was taken away to be incarcerated in the *Académie française des aliénés*.

A source within the *Académie* provided routine updates to the tabloid including details of the sergeant's life within the horrid place including a disturbing report that he spent most of his days in a strait jacket screaming various iterations of the following:

"It was the damned alcoholics from America, that's who!"

Gregg looked at Trey.

"Is that us? Gregg asked.

"Duh," Trey said. "I'd say we're on the short list."

The story did not identify the alcoholic Americans accused by the deranged sergeant of this heinous crime, but it reported that the authorities in France and Great Britain knew their identities and would certainly like to have a chat over spot of tea or glass of white Burgundian wine with them if they ever stepped foot on British or French soil. The words "detain", "interrogate" or "arrest" were never mentioned.

But it didn't sound good.

Gregg looked pale.

"Elisabeth and I are going to Ireland next month," he cried. "Does that count? Is that Britain? I sure don't want to end up in the Tower of London getting my head chopped off. I would look it up but my internet isn't working right now. Or maybe it's my ethernet. Who can tell? What's the difference?"

Trey looked at Gregg like he was crazy.

"You think you've got problems," Trey said, panic and bile rising in his throat in equal measures. "Leeza and I are going to French Polynesia next year and I don't know if that's really French or if they just stole the name. Who can figure this out?"

Gregg said, "While I've got your iPad, I'll look it up."

Trey grabbed his iPad way from his friend and clutched it to his chest fearful that Gregg would accidentally touch a series of random keys that would render his device inoperable.

"You know what," Trey said. "We've gotten away with murder, literally and figuratively. It was entirely accidental, as we all agree. Let's just make sure we vacation from now on where they can't get us."

"Excellent plan," Gregg said. "I'm glad you're thinking straight for a change."

PART VII

After several days of relaxing on the beach and drinking cocktails with little umbrellas, the two couples decided it was time to take a tour of the exotic island where they were vacationing.

They arranged a private car and a local guide to drive them around for a day that included stops at secluded and private beaches. At one of the beaches, an elegant lunch and a variety of wines had been arranged by a local restaurant and was served on the sand under a palm tree. It was extraordinary.

To make it even better, there was no cell service for most of the day so no one could be disturbed. It didn't matter to Gregg, who hadn't had cell service since he pulled out of his driveway a week earlier.

As the day drew to its satisfying conclusion, the two couples got into the little black van for the winding trip back to their luxury hotel where they hoped to arrive in time to watch the Caribbean sun set at a tiny tiki bar that faced the western sky and was famous for its sundowner cocktails.

The foursome was whetting its appetite for the refreshing cocktails and happily chatting about plans for another day on the sparkling beach as the van meandered through the island on narrow streets lined by picture postcard palm trees swaying in the gentle coastal breeze.

Without slowing, the van drove past the entrance to their hotel.

"Uh, excuse me," Trey said, whipping around his head, which made him slightly carsick after the lunchtime indulgences of excellent wine. "Wasn't that our hotel?"

The van sped up.

The driver and guide sitting next to him said nothing.

The passengers stopped talking and looked at Trey, who shrugged his shoulders.

"Perhaps they're taking us someplace for a special drink or something," he said.

They headed for the downtown area.

"Hey guys, what's up? We want to get back to see the sunset," Gregg said nervously.

More silence from the front seat.

The van came to a quick halt in front of a small cinder block building.

It sure didn't look like a tourist spot or place to have a cool and comforting beverage.

It didn't look fun at all.

"Oh shit," Trey said, pointing to the sign on the building, "Look at that."

Turks and Caicos Government Headquarters
A Proud British Overseas Territory

The passengers gasped in unison.

"You're a total numbskull," Gregg said to Trey as Gregg jiggled the locked door handle trying to find an escape.

"Were you just going to leave us?" Elisabeth asked her husband as he desperately pushed against the unyielding door and jabbed at the window with his elbow, accomplishing nothing but injuring himself.

"I was thinking about it," said Gregg, still jiggling.

"Good gracious," Trey said. "I thought we'd be safe here. Who knew this was British?"

"Probably the entire world," said Leeza derisively. "Nice job, you idiot."

The van door slid open, revealing a tall man in a military uniform, all sorts of medals and decorations on this chest, a sidearm on his belt.

"Welcome," he said, sounding like the villain in a James Bond flick. "We've been expecting you. Please, if you will, follow me."

The four passengers stepped from the van.

"Come with me," said the bemedaled tall man.

They entered the dark and smelly building and were guided to a tiny room with no windows, a small video camera with a blinking red light pointed at them.

"I was asked to have a spot of tea with you," said their well-decorated host.

Everyone held their breath. There was no tea. Gregg smoothed his hair for the camera.

"Our British overlords want to know if you remember Brian and Hilary," he continued.

"Who?" Trey asked.

Their uniformed captor smiled.

"You know very well who," he said menacingly, no longer smiling.

"I knew this was going to happen," Gregg snarled, glaring at Trey. "I read about this kind of stuff on the internet when I had a signal three years ago."

The tall man surveyed the terrified group in the tiny room. He slowly looked from one frightened face to the other.

"The American alcoholics," he said grinning. "I am so happy to finally meet you. I've heard much about you. And of all the colonies in the world held hostage by the British, you wandered into mine."

Nobody said anything. Nobody was even breathing.

"I'll tell you what," he said, moving behind the small camera and pushing a button. The red light stopped blinking.

"One thousand American dollars. On this table. Now. And you'll see your sunset tonight."

The four Americans looked at each other.

"What will you tell the British government?" Trey asked, his voice trembling.

"You let me worry about them," he said with a huge grin. "They think they know everything and are masters of the world but they're idiots just like those lugs who ended up dead in that French canal."

He continued.

"I will step out for ten minutes. When I return, I will count what is on the table and that will determine what happens next."

He left and locked the door.

The four American alcoholics looked at each other.

Leeza immediately dug into her purse, all the while glaring at Trey. Three hundred dollars.

Trey pulled four hundred from a secret wallet designed to deter pickpockets.

Gregg added thirty-seven cents.

Elisabeth, thankfully, had exactly enough to meet the tall man's demand.

They piled the money on the table and counted it three times.

One thousand dollars and thirty-seven cents.

Trey banged on the door.

The tall man entered the room and casually counted the cash to make sure the amount was correct. He ignored Gregg's loose change.

He opened the door and pointed to it.

"Get out of here," he said, a broad grin on his face. "There's a sunset awaiting you!

"And the next time you lose patience with someone, count your pills more carefully!"

THE END

AUTHOR'S NOTES

Some of my faithful readers may recognize parts of this novel – or think they're having a déjà vu moment. The story of the train wreck during the log-loading scene is adapted from a tale that first appeared in my virtually unread collection of short stories, "Vanessa". Since hardly anyone read "Vanessa", I was confident that most readers would read this scene here for the first time.

As with all my stories, this is not a history book so no complaining or nitpicking. I did no research on the history of trains such as when the railroads switched from steam locomotives to diesel electrics and my descriptions of the transportation of cigarette products are entirely fabricated even though the cigarettes didn't move themselves. I have no idea how many cigarettes are in a boxcar, so I just made up the numbers.

What is entirely accurate is my depiction of life on a mill hill which, in this novel, is based on the real-life neighborhood that housed the workers at Erwin Mills in Durham, a major textile manufacturer of its day. During my teen years, I delivered the afternoon paper, the Durham Sun, six days a week to these people many of whom stood on their porches waiting for my arrival and their daily entertainment. They subscribed to the afternoon newspaper because they went to work so early they had no time for the morning paper. I collected forty cents from them every Saturday morning. It was heartbreaking to watch them search their coin purses for enough to pay the bill. And, later that day, I'd ride my bike back through the same dirt streets to bring them their Saturday afternoon paper even to those who couldn't pay the bill that week. These were the kindest people I've ever known. They spent their entire adult lives doing hard, mindless jobs and living in a tiny world from which most never escaped. And enjoying the afternoon newspaper. It's taken me a lifetime to appreciate my small role in making their lives better.

As always, I'm deeply grateful to those who read my nonsense in its draft form and point out the errors, the continuity problems and storylines that make no sense. The first set of eyes always belong to my wife Lisa Piercy, whose opinions, suggestions and encouragement are critical. She read an early draft of one segment of this book and pronounced it "the craziest thing I've ever read," so I knew I was on the right track. My sister Kay and her husband Nate always offer ways to improve my stories and I appreciate their enthusiasm and suggestions. Barbara Reining reads more books than anyone I know and is always graciously willing to read my drafts and tell me what she thinks. The contributions of all these people are in these pages and the book is so much better than it was before they reviewed it.

Anne Piercy, to whom this book is dedicated, is my biggest fan and always is itching to get her hands on the latest copy of whatever I write. Her enthusiasm inspires me immensely.

I'm also always deeply grateful to Kimberly Daniels Taws, the owner of The Country Bookshop in Southern Pines, NC, for putting my books on her shelves and for her unwavering support of local authors. One day I hope to surprise us both by actually selling a book.

I'd also like to thank Melissa Fallon for sharing the wonderful stories about her mother that were the inspiration to feature unfiltered Camel cigarettes in the book.

The short story, "Chaos in the Canal," was written for fun and to entertain my traveling companions on a barge cruise in France. The first very short draft was written for laughs while we were on the barge and then later expanded into the nonsense you have in your hands. It is a work of fiction! No one died on our barge cruise! But it was a close call!

This is my third book with the team at Firebrand Publishing, and I always appreciate the professionalism and patience of Amy Cancryn and her editors and proofreaders who make every sentence better.

Finally, it was also noted, astutely, that I am addicted to commas, and it was suggested, by several who read the drafts, that I remove perhaps one thousand of them, or more, which I did, happily.

ABOUT THE AUTHOR

Gene Upchurch is a native of Durham and a graduate of the University of North Carolina at Chapel Hill.

He was a sportswriter before embarking on a 28-year career in public affairs, community relations, and legislative advocacy in the utility industry. He is a proud recipient of the Order of the Long Leaf Pine, the State of North Carolina's highest civilian honor.

His previous novels, "The Eno Club" and "Burnt", have not been international bestsellers nor was his collection of short stories, "Vanessa". Hope springs eternal.

He lives in Pinehurst, North Carolina, with his wife, Lisa.

www.ingramcontent.com/pod-product-compliance
Lightning Source LLC
Chambersburg PA
CBHW010448310726
48979CB00018B/2859/J

* 9 7 8 1 9 4 1 9 0 7 6 9 6 *